LEASHED

Zoe Dawson

BLUE
MOON
CREATIVE
LLC
write • paint • create

Find Zoe Dawson on the web!
www.zoedawson.com

Cover design by Robyn Ludwig at Robin Ludwig Design, Inc.
Editing Services provided by Faith Freewoman and proofing by Judy DeVries
Interior Design by Penoaks Publishing, http://penoaks.com

ISBN: 978-0-9913515-3-4

PRAISE FOR LEASHED

"Leashed is a super-sweet, quick and easy read that had be smiling from start to finish! Zoe Dawson cleverly introduces her Going to the Dogs series with this fun book that features Callie and Owen, and their dogs Jack and Jill. See? Even the dogs have super-sweet names. This is a well-written, fast-paced read with an HEA. Leashed will appeal to a wide variety of readers including animal lovers, romance lovers, and anyone just looking for a fun read. Well done Zoe Dawson; you have created a super-fan who will sing the praises of your work far and wide. Woof!!"

– RoloPoloBookBlog

"I just could not put this book down so read it in one sitting till 2am. Everything about it was just AWESOME!! The cover, the story. I could go on and on... The characters were so meant to be and their pets knew it from the very start. I have never seen two people so set on not falling for each other. I was quite sad when I read the last page. Five stars and two thumbs way up for Zoe Dawson. Wooot Wooot!! ;)"

– Kindle Customer.

"A great and moving romance that has it all. Great characters you can't help but love, and situations that will melt your heart one minute and make you laugh out loud in another. Callie is a dog trainer with a past of broken hearts by bad boys and owns a Great Dane named Jack. Owen is her neighbor, a club owner with a bad boy reputation, and his Great Dane is Jill. Jack knocks up Jill and the adventure begins. The chemistry between Callie and Owen is enough to steam up any room. I thoroughly enjoyed this book and couldn't put it down. Now I'm dying to get my hands on the next one."

– Larisa Edwards

ACKNOWLEDGMENTS

I'd like to thank Sarra Cannon for all her encouragement and support as I embark on this self-publishing adventure. I owe a debt of gratitude to both Bridget Foy for believing in me and Dare Cook for her beta reading. Thank you, also, to Faith Freewoman for her excellent advice and editing skills.

CHAPTER ONE

A WOMAN'S LAUGHTER drifted into the hall as Callie Lassiter trudged home. She glared at Owen McKay's door as she slipped her key into the lock of her trendy Tribeca loft. Sounded like Owen was having much more fun on his date than she'd had on hers.

Yep, another dating disaster. Okay, so not as much a disaster as a ho-hum snooze fest. With an inner sigh, she reflected on this evening's dating fiasco. He was nice. Quite nice, but he might as well have been an amoeba, because she'd felt no attraction. None. When had dating become so…rote?

Since she decided a man with an edge was not an option. Yep, she was a bad boy junkie, but often addictive things were just plain not good for you. Like chocolate. Also not good for you. Still, Callie couldn't help but feel let down.

The laughter tinkled again, sweet and clear. Envy twisted in her stomach and pressed against her chest. She threw his door another glare. She bet the woman Owen was entertaining looked like one of those high-fashion models she usually saw hanging on his arm in the *New York Scoop* photos she pretended not to notice. The guy was gorgeous; of course he would only date high-quality arm candy, never a girl-next-door type like Callie.

She was a tomboy and passionate about it. She'd rather be climbing, surfing, diving, skiing, playing basketball with her brother and his friends, or running than attend snooty parties or shopping. Much to her friend Harper's dismay.

He also had to keep up appearances. As one of Manhattan's players, he owned FLASH, a classy nightclub that everyone in the city considered *the* place to see and be seen. He was often reported to be with a different woman each week. But even his stylish clothes and expensive, hip haircut couldn't disguise his true nature. And she'd learned the hard way that untamable, audacious, and daring meant bad boy with capital Bs.

At least there was one male eager to see her, one she could depend on, and who was always excited to greet her as she came through the door. And this enormous boy wasn't at all boring.

Pushing the door open, she braced herself for her exuberant but well-trained Great Dane, Jack. He was right there to greet her, as always, and Callie kissed him on the bridge of his black and white nose.

She deposited her Judith Leiber vintage clutch on the hall table and gave her full attention to Jack.

He filled the doorway with his big body. Every time they did their welcome-home ritual, she was grateful for the first skill she had taught Jack—not to jump up. With a dog this large, it would be unpleasant, and could be dangerous to small children.

"Hi there, Jack! Who's a good boy?" Callie cooed as she stroked Jack's head and rubbed all over his silky fur. She wouldn't be able to get past this cheerful, affectionate two-hundred-pound bundle of canine energy without first paying the entry fee of a big dose of love, which she did gladly.

She was having so much fun with Jack that she barely noticed a door open down the hall, followed by a brief conversation before the door closed and footsteps retreated toward the elevator.

Grabbing Jack's leash, she clipped it to his collar, headed back out the door, and locked it behind them. She enjoyed their walks as much as he did, and did them as often as her busy business allowed. And since she was the boss and owner of Sit Happens, an obedience and dog training business on the Lower East Side, she could build her schedule to suit her needs, and Jack's. "I had a really disappointing date," Callie confided as they headed down the hall.

Jack's ears pricked and he made a comforting sound. Then, prancing with excitement, he proceeded to get tangled in his leash. As Callie bent down to unravel him, she heard a most unwelcome voice behind her.

"Your Dane is big enough to be a pinto, and he has the right two-tone coloring."

Callie's bad boy meter shot up into the red zone. Owen McKay *would* have to mock her. There he stood in all his glory, just outside his loft door, his hip cocked and his intent eyes studying her. Naturally, Owen lived in the most modern and sleek of all the lofts her brother and his outrageously creative friends had produced. As if his clothes were a natural extension of his upscale residence, he had on a black crewneck sweater and a pair of sinfully tight black pants, accentuating narrow hips and hard, strong-looking thighs. His come-hither eyes traveled slowly over her, and she realized that she was staring and holding her breath.

Instructing herself to snap out of it, she mentally reiterated her vow never to get involved with another man who was dangerous, unpredictable, a rebel who didn't care whose feelings got hurt. Callie firmly reminded herself why she had stopped dating selfish and emotionally unavailable men. She was the one who usually got hurt.

Owen McKay came with so many danger-Will-Robinson complications she had no intention of opening that Pandora's Box.

She straightened and stood for a moment in silent agony. *Why* did she become speechless every time she saw Owen? Thank God it only happened with him, or she'd be out of business in a week!

"His markings are referred to as Harlequin." Oh, my God! Did that nonsense come out of *her* mouth in that stuffy, schoolmarmish-correcting-the-student-tone? She should find a comfortable and quiet spot to bang her head repeatedly against the wall. Hard.

He smiled as if he was indulging her. "I know."

A big, dark muzzle pushed its way out of his half-open loft door. The big body came after, the dog's tail wagging so hard her whole body shook.

"Ah, another Dane lover." Then he probably wasn't all bad. Maybe.

Owen reached inside the door and grabbed a leash, then closed and locked his door. "Yes, I am. I'm Owen McKay, by the way, and this is Jill." He clipped the leash to the black and white bitch's collar. "Time for your walk, girl."

"No way."

He shot her a puzzled look.

"Meet Jack. And I'm Callie Lassiter," she said with a grin.

Owen laughed, and it was like a rich, decadent dessert. Incredibly tempting and probably very bad for her.

At the moment she was distracted by Owen's hot-fudge-sundae laugh, Jack made a totally unexpected, lightning move, all the while crooning a soft woofing noise deep in his throat. "Jack, heel!"

Jack merely jerked the leash out of her hand as he bolted for the pretty female.

Her dog's completely uncharacteristic behavior left her speechless, and, for critical seconds, completely at a loss.

"Jack!"

Jill coyly sidestepped Jack as Callie zipped down the hall and caught her dog's collar, but moving two hundred unwilling pounds was impossible. "Jack, *sit!*"

Incredibly, he ignored her again.

In the meantime, Jill danced around her master with Jack in hot pursuit. Jill's leash wrapped around Owen, and then around Callie, at the same time that Jack's loose leash got snagged around their ankles. In moments they were completely entangled with the dogs and with each other.

The clinging black crewneck shirt he wore felt soft under her fingers as she clutched him for balance. His pecs were thick and hard, his scent and physicality making her feel weak in the knees while her insides melted into a gooey mess.

This close, she could see that his irises were a vivid blue, shot with deep gold and rimmed in black. His eyes were intense and compelling, and she felt her interest in him deepen. Damn!

In spite of the canine commotion surrounding them, she could not shake off this man's spell. At least she couldn't until she felt the leashes tighten and yank her off-balance and into a tangled heap with Owen on top.

And then her brain seized up completely when one of those hard thighs pushed between her legs and that flat stomach came up against hers.

For a suspended moment she took in his gorgeous, masculine features back-dropped by thick brown hair that was mussed and sexy. His mouth was close to hers, lips pursed and so sensual. Her mouth tingled and ached with wondering what they would feel like against hers. Almost as though he also could feel the magnetic connection vibrating between her mouth and his, he angled his head toward her, his eyes on her lips.

His lazy smile captivated her, coiling low and deep inside. And she could feel herself softening, heating, pulsing with a need to press against his thigh, which was parked so temptingly close to her center.

She heard a woof in the distance and something prodded her with the impression that the sound was important. When it grew more distant, she snapped out of her daze.

"Jack!"

"Jill!"

Owen moved off her quickly, but the hall was empty and the door to the stairs was wide open.

"Holy crap!" Callie shouted as she took off down the hall. When she reached the stairs, she saw Jill's leash and broken collar. "She must have gotten it caught on the railing. Damn, Owen. Without her tags it'll be hard to identify her."

"Don't worry. She has one of those ID chips. Thanks for caring, though."

The warmth of his voice made her sigh softly, in spite of her desperation to find Jack before something happened to her precious two-year-old.

"Jack does, too," she said breathlessly as they raced down to the lobby, but the dogs were nowhere to be found. Callie covered her mouth, fighting tears. She ran out the door and into the street.

"How do you think they got out? This is so unlike Jack. He never runs away."

"Jill's gotten away from me a couple of times."

"Jack!" Callie called. "Come!"

She took off down West Broadway towards the Hudson River with a lump in her throat that was pure fear. Where *was* he? This street led directly to the Hudson, and he could be hit by a car, or catch his paw in a pothole, or any number of other dangers that could befall her precious baby.

Night had fallen, and even though streetlights illuminated the sidewalks, it was slow going. They stopped people as they passed, asking them if they'd seen the two Danes. After she and Owen searched corners and doorways and alleys for more than an hour, they decided to return home and see if the dogs had found their way back.

"I can't believe this." Callie felt tears welling again as they finally reached their building. "I'm going to call the recovery company right now."

Owen touched her arm, a comforting warmth. "I'm sure it won't take long to find him then."

"I hope so. He's never been alone in this city…"

But when they walked into the building, both their rascals were cozied up next to the elevator, their big heads snugly nestled on each other's bodies.

"Jack!" Callie called, so happy to see him she didn't even scold.

He got up and came trotting over. She wrapped her arms around his neck and hugged him. "It's getting late, but he still needs a walk," she said to herself.

"So does Jill. Could you keep her occupied until I run upstairs and get her other collar and leash?"

"No problem."

While Callie waited for Owen to come back, she struggled to shut out memories of the hot, etched-permanently-in-her-mind night she'd once spent with a sexy bad boy who'd encouraged her to be as reckless and wicked as she dared. But, she firmly reminded herself, she'd grown up, left that phase of her life after one too many emotionally unavailable men. Her sexy neighbor was off-limits. Totally. Off. Limits.

The moment in the hallway when his body had been pressed to hers was incredibly sensual, though… It had made her remember what it had been like to experience that twist of excitement, that overwhelming attraction that made her want to risk her safety and her sanity just to get close to a man.

When Owen came back downstairs, he was wearing a light coat and an air of detachment that effectively obliterated her budding fantasies.

"Thanks," he said, slipping the collar over Jill's head. "It was nice to finally meet you."

"Yes, we're now well acquainted." Oh, my God! How lame that sounded. Where *was* that head-banging wall anyway?

As Owen moved past her towards the front door, Jack whined. Callie kept a tight hand on his collar and waited until Owen was out the door and had turned down the street before following.

"Yeah," Callie said softly, her eyes on Owen, but her words were for Jack's ears only. "I know exactly how you feel."

"Someone just walked into her apartment and took it right off the couch."

"A pillow?"

"That's what I heard. But, her door was unlocked. Her husband had just run downstairs for a paper. Lesson learned. I'd say."

"What would a thief want with a pillow?"

Callie didn't wait to hear the answer as she ushered Jack toward the door and past two women talking next to the mailboxes. Today Jack was behaving like his old self, instantly obeying her every command.

They crossed West Broadway at the traffic light and walked until she reached the Union Square Dog Run. Brooke Palmer was already there with her bulldog Roscoe. Waving to Brooke, Callie went through the gate and closed it behind her, latching it securely.

"Hey," Brooke said to Callie, and then to Jack, "how's my big boy?" She rubbed Jack's head. "When are you bringing him in again for grooming?" Brooke owned Pawlish, a high-end dog spa that catered to the wealthy dog owners of Manhattan. She was presently in the middle of an impressive expansion to her business.

Roscoe and Jack sniffed each other and then ran off to wrestle around together. "Next week. I don't think I can fit it in this week. My schedule is too full." Callie sat, crossing her legs as she leaned back against the park bench.

"He's always so well-behaved, not like Kristen Davis-Wright's fidgety poodle. I wish that woman would take her dog somewhere else," Brooke said, pushing back her dark hair in exasperation. "Where are you off to this week? Rock climbing, a quick trip to the Swiss Alps for skiing, hang gliding off the side of a mountain? I swear you scare the living daylights out of me. I'd have a hard enough time climbing the rock wall at my gym and that's because of your influence."

"It's rock climbing and hiking. I have to get out of the city and do something physical every week. I'm going to Breakneck Ridge Trail."

"That doesn't sound very safe."

"It's totally safe. It's a nine-and-a-half-mile loop, but I'll be doing just about two miles of it. It's too steep to bring Jack. He'll have to wait until the following week for his long hike. It's got exactly what I like, steep ascensions, some rock climbing, and the scenery…it's breathtaking. I'm thinking of booking a trip to Cabo San Lucas. I hear the cliff diving is amazing."

Brooke smiled and clasped Callie's wrist. "You are a daredevil and much braver than I am."

Just then Harper Sinclair and her standard poodle, Blue, entered the park. Harper released her dog and watched her race off to meet up with Roscoe and Jack, but not before Callie noticed the sparkling collar around Blue's neck.

Harper's grandfather owned large parcels of land in the city and had made a large fortune from both selling land and developing it. His moneymaking talents had obviously been inherited by her friend. Case in point her poodle's undoubtedly diamond-studded collar. The poodle was a best-in-show blue-ribbon moneymaker, but Harper never treated her like anything but a dog. No pampering for Edgewood Sky High Blue.

Her pedigree was clear in the exquisite lines of the poodle's solid body, but Blue's registered name always made Callie smile. It was derived from her sire, Topgun, and the dam's name of

Freefalling–resulting in Sky High Blue. Or Blue for short. And, champion or not, the dark poodle joined right in with the ruckus.

"What's going on with the bling?" Callie asked.

Harper sighed. "Grandmother Sinclair strikes again. She's staying with me for a few days. She made me put it on Blue before we left."

"It's real? A diamond dog collar?" Brooke asked, an incredulous look on her face. "I *thought* Wright-Davis was overindulgent."

"Yes, fifty thou worth. Can you imagine walking your dog around Manhattan with that thing around her neck? Grandmother Sinclair is a few diamonds short in her tiara. Hopefully people will think it's fake. But, if I were mugged, I'd give them the damn thing. I don't think Blue likes it much."

"For your safety, you should leave it at home," Brooke advised.

"I can only try," Harper said. "By the way, ladies, whose idea was it to meet at eight-thirty on a Saturday morning?" Harper groused. In her Vuitton coat and designer sunglasses, she looked like a rich snoot, but Harper was as down to earth as dirt.

"Scoot over, I'm bushed, too much party and not enough sleep," she said, working her way onto the bench between Callie and Brooke.

"My heart bleeds for you," Callie offered sarcastically.

"Social climbing is a full-time job," Harper said, flashing a wily grin. She shrugged out of her caramel and cream coat, fluffing up her golden locks.

"Right," Brooke look worried. "Callie is more into *rock* climbing and she's going to break her neck next week."

"What?" Harper said, a puzzled and concerned look on her face.

"It's Breakneck Ridge Trail," Callie laughed and nudged Brooke.

Brooke laughed and Harper gave Callie the same kind of look most people gave her who weren't into a sporty lifestyle—incredulous.

Brooke continued. "And I seem to recall that it was your idea to meet at this hour."

Harper paused in mid-fluff, turning to look at Brooke. "Was I sober at the time?"

"I think so," Brooke said, smiling indulgently.

"Well, damn. I guess I should realize I need my beauty sleep before blurting out ungodly meeting times."

"Are you already picking on Harper?" Poe Madigan asked from behind them as she followed her Jack Russell terriers, affectionately known as The Terrible Two for short. They came trotting into the park like they owned it. Edgar and Allan were notorious little brats.

Poe settled on the bench next to Callie as her dogs raced off. Poe was aptly named, with her blue-streaked hair, raven tattoo, and the whole Goth vibe. She planned to open a veterinary practice when her hospital internship was completed in the spring, and Callie was sure Poe's Cornell DVM would guarantee plenty of patients.

"Harper brings it on herself," Brooke said, picking up the interrupted thread.

"I need to get a second job. New York is so much more expensive than Ithaca," Poe announced, her face showing that she was already stressed about it.

"Oh, sweetie, I can help."

"No, Harper, it's not up to you to support me. I can make my own way. I didn't bring it up to get sympathy. I just wanted to let you all know that I might not make it some Saturdays for our play date."

"I don't like the sound of that," Callie said. "We'll miss you and the two terribles." Callie slipped her arm around her friend's shoulder and squeezed, giving her a reassuring smile.

"I don't know what kind of schedule I'll have, so don't worry yet. Thanks, though." Poe returned the smile and squeezed Callie's hand, then wrapped her arm around Harper's shoulders to give her a quick hug.

"Not to change the subject, Poe, but how did your first laser surgery go?" Brooke asked.

"Great. It was fascinating, and Dr. Martin let me do everything while he supervised. I can't wait to do another one."

"Would that be the cute Dr. Martin?"

Poe blushed and looked away. "He's pretty cute."

"Ask him out," Harper urged.

"No. That's not my thing. A guy should ask a woman out. Besides, I'm afraid I'll just make some obscure reference. He'll stare at me and not know what to say. Then, I'll say something even worse. Then we'll find it awkward whenever we're together at work. Or he'll just look at me and realize I'm a geek."

"My date last night almost put me to sleep," Callie said.

"How disappointing. But I can top that. I got a text from Sam, the guy I've been dating for a week. He said, and I quote, 'Can I reserve u for our next date?' Reserve me? What am I? A restaurant?" Brooke asked.

"Did he spell out *you?*" Poe asked.

"Nope. Used 'u' like we're still in high school. What is it with guys who can't spell out you? It's not like the phone company charges you per letter," Brooke said.

"It's just plain lazy," Poe chimed in.

"The boring date was something I could handle, but I had a close encounter with *Mr. Gorgeous.*"

"Owen McKay. He's bad news. A love 'em and leave 'em bad boy," Brooke said. "You've read the *New York Scoop.*"

"I know, but every time I get near him, I lose it. He has a Mantle Great Dane, mostly black, that Jack lusted after to the point where he completely ignored me and yanked his leash out of my hand. That dog of his could really benefit from some training."

"Callie, you're getting off topic," Brooke pointed out.

"Sorry. His dog tripped us, and we ended up on the floor and Mr. Gorgeous landed on top of me with his thigh right between my legs."

"Owen is great in bed," Harper said.

All conversation stopped while the group turned in unison to look at her. Harper laughed. "Oh! No! Don't look at me like that. I didn't get naked with him. I just heard that."

"That's a relief," Callie said. "Wait. What am I saying? I got myself hurt constantly in college by all the bad boys I dated. It wouldn't be smart to get involved with Owen. It would have been better if you *had* been intimate with him."

Even though Callie acknowledged that Owen probably was a bad bet, she was secretly very glad Harper hadn't done the deed with him. It would make him off limits, and part of her wasn't against that, but another naughtier and less reasonable part of her was giddy.

"I don't want to sleep with him, but you do," Harper said smugly.

"He makes me melt." All three women groaned. "I know, but it's true."

"You're smart to steer clear. Emotionally unavailable men don't change," Brooke said. "Now don't give me that sad face. It's for your own good."

"But we all wish they would change," Poe said wistfully.

Callie couldn't agree more.

Just then Edgar ran up to a little girl who was holding an ice cream cone. Just as she bent down to pet him, Allan swooped in and stole the treat.

"Edgar and Allan," Poe scolded. "I've told you no team tagging children!"

The Terrible Two ran off to enjoy the spoils and all four women broke out into laughter. Poe made amends by buying the little girl another cone and warned her to keep away from the little varmints.

In the middle of the week, Callie got up early, packed up what she would need for her hike and got into the elevator that would bring her down to the parking garage and her lime green Jeep. She was used to and comfortable driving in the city, navigating the traffic, and the hundreds of yellow cabs. She drove to West 79th Street and from there took Palisades Interstate Parkway north. An hour and a few minutes later, she was turning into the parking lot on Breakneck Road near Cold Springs, New York.

Grabbing her backpack, she slipped into the straps and headed to the southern end of the parking area just north of the tunnel, heading south. She immediately reached a viewpoint over the Hudson River to the left of the trail. Storm King Mountain was visible directly across the river, and Bannerman's Castle on Pollepel Island was to the right.

She pulled out a bottle of water from her pack and opened it, taking a sip, but immediately blew it out when she heard Own McKay's deep voice. "Hello, Callie."

She jerked around to find him standing behind her, a pack of his own, the wind blowing through his thick brown hair, those blue eyes taking her in.

"Owen. What brings you out here?" She devoured him with one big gulp from his red T-shirt, hugging every delicious muscle on his chest and abdomen, cinching his lean waist to the black cargo shorts and hiking boots, all top of the line.

"Now I know who dropped the brochure for this place in the hall. Must have been you."

"That's what happened to it? I like going over the trails and deciding which route to take. You've never been out here? It's a pretty strenuous hike."

He smiled and it seemed the wattage was enough to melt bones. She wasn't sure how she was going to hike with no internal skeleton. "No, but I've trekked Blue Mountain Reservation Loop and been to places around the world. Does that count?"

"I didn't mean you looked soft...you don't. Ah, you look hard. Tough as nails." Oh my gerd, could she be any more of a tongue-tied idiot? Apparently, her confidence seemed to desert her whenever *Mr. Gorgeous* was anywhere in the vicinity.

His smile widened at the way she tripped over her words and she sternly told herself to get-a-freaking-grip.

"You don't think a night club owner can keep up with you, Ms. Lassiter," he murmured. The wind playing with his hair the way she wanted to. He raised his brows. "I think I can give you a run for your money. Shall we?"

She stared at him for a moment. Was he actually going on this hike with her? Somehow, she found herself on an impromptu date with the bad boy next door. None of her friends would approve. But she couldn't back down now. She'd just challenged him. Of all the wrong places, wrong time coincidences.

"Maybe you won't be able to keep up with me."

Oh-ho, now he was definitely challenging her and that was something she couldn't tolerate. Callie's competitive nature wouldn't let her back down now. She straightened her shoulders, narrowed her eyes and said, "Let's go."

CHAPTER TWO

THE UNIVERSE WAS LAUGHING at him right now. Rolling-around-on-the-floor-laughing. It was his intention to avoid this put together beauty-next-door with her sweet vibe, easy-going manner, and killer bod.

His eyes slid over her, from her golden-brown hair down to her serviceable, black leather hiking boots. Her hair was pulled back and threaded through a baseball cap that looked adorable on her. She wore a blue top and a pair of stretchy black shorts that hit about mid-thigh of her toned, shapely legs, fit snug at her slim waist, and hugged her spectacular hiney. He was a master at reading body language, especially female body language, and even as his eyes returned to her face, he noticed how she leaned toward him. He was sure she wasn't even aware of it. It made his blood heat to a slow burn.

He needed cold water right now, but on this warm September day in the middle of nowhere, he wasn't going to get it. The best he could hope for was something to distract him. He looked to the cliff she started walking toward. Excellent. That would do.

But when they started to climb, he was right below that spectacular ass and he had to concentrate on where he was putting his hands and feet. Yeah, he knew where he wanted to put his hands.

Focus man. She's much too sweet for you.

Besides, Callie was the kind of girl who knew how to get secrets out of a man without even trying. She was one of those women who listened and was invested and involved in what a guy was saying. Not the arm candy type he often dated and forgot the next day.

There wasn't a thing he wanted to remember about his past except how his great aunt had taken him in and nurtured him. His throat got tight thinking about her. She had passed away not more than five weeks ago and the grief would hit him out of the blue. Still much too fresh. He was once again alone in the world, well, except for Jill.

He averted his eyes to right in front of him as he took care in making sure he was well placed before pushing up to the next handholds. Callie was fast and nimble. It was clear she was a natural at climbing and had done it often. She had the kind of athletic, muscled body that he usually dismissed. Not because he wasn't completely lusting after it, but women like Callie had much, too much in common with him.

He tended to be a loner on his treks and he liked it that way.

He looked to his left and noticed the amazing scenery through the trees, their leaves rustling in the light breeze.

After about twenty minutes of climbing, they reached a rock ledge marked by a flagpole and after that a vantage point to take a breather and enjoy the views.

"It's hard to believe we're not far from Megatropolis."

Callie chuckled as she sat down on the cliff's outcropping and pulled out a bottle of water. Owen did the same, parched from the exertion of the climb.

She took a healthy swig and Owen wondered if she was one of those women that really enjoyed her food, wondering how healthy her appetite was in other ways as well. He almost wanted to ask her out to dinner to see if she was one of those pickers he hated or a chow hound which he much preferred.

But, no, dinner would lead to something else, and something else that would then make him hurt her. She lived next door and it was smart not to screw up his living arrangement. He loved that loft, spacious and beautifully built.

"Megatropolis? Makes New York City sound like a comic book rendition of a big city—like Gotham."

"Yeah, it's a beast but I love it. I grew up...there." Yeah, that was for sure. He'd grown up fast. What was it about this girl that had almost made him say he'd grown up on the streets? He never talked about it, not even by accident.

"Yeah, get this, kids actually ride their bikes around here and get out of the house. Radical, huh? I know because I grew up in Harrison, not far from here."

He pulled his eyes from her as she took off her cap and resituated her long tail of hair. He tried to enjoy the sun-dappled Hudson, the blue smudged Catskills in the distance. But when she pulled off the blue shirt, then reseated the cap, revealing a gray sports bra beneath, firmly hugging her generous breasts, his attention lasered right back to her. His mouth went a little dry at her creamy skin, the smooth satin of her shoulders. "Shoot, I should probably put it back on. I'll burn."

She reached for her shirt and like a freaking moron," he said, "I have sunscreen. I can put it on for you."

She eyed him like he was suddenly a black bear who had materialized out of the forest. And she should be wary, he was a predator, and she was one tasty looking morsel.

"Oh, um, okay. It's pretty hot."

That was an understatement. Now committed to keep her beautiful skin from burning, he reached for his pack, but she already had a tube in her hand. "I have some, too." She held up a can of bug spray, the deep woods kind. "And tick repellent. Do you mind?"

He cleared his throat, but his voice came out compressed anyway. "No. Of course not."

Yeah, right, of course he didn't mind rubbing cream all over her back. What was to mind? He took the tube and squirted some into his hands and rubbed them together, she turned so he could have easy access to her back. With an inhale of air, he set his palms against her. Well, of course he'd been right. There was nothing whatsoever to mind about helping her out with this simple task. The soft skin, the firm muscles, the heat from her that penetrated through his pores into his bloodstream, making his heart beat double time, making him feel like a randy sixteen-year-old boy. He got hard just like a teenager.

"Rub it in good," she murmured.

He closed his eyes and realized he hadn't released his breath. He exhaled, thinking they were out in the wide-open spaces. Why did it feel like there wasn't enough oxygen to go around?

He made small circles, using his thumbs against those nice muscles. Did he really like softer women better? It wasn't as if her skin wasn't like silk over the firmness. He moved up to her shoulders, her skin glistening with the properties of the sunscreen, then up the back of her neck, her silky hair brushing against the backs of his hands. She shivered and made a small, soft sound that went through him like a heated wave and only made his balls tighten.

He should remove his hands and get his shit under control, but he still had to do her lower back. He licked his lips. Damn he loved the sight of the small of a woman's back. He switched to rubbing in the cream there and she let out another one of those little gasps, then a mmhmm. He made sure to do a thorough job, not sure if it was because he so enjoyed touching her or because he was trying to do a thorough job.

Then he was done and thank God. He moved away for her and wiped his hands down his legs to get rid of the excess sunscreen. He picked up the spray and gave her back a good dousing.

Her voice was breathless when she said, "Thank you." She took care of her arms and chest and mouth-watering midriff while he tried not to stare. "We should get going." She tucked the shirt and sunscreen into her backpack and stood up. He followed suit.

They came to the next cliff face and there was a white X on the rock with arrows right and left. She turned to him. "Easy or hard?" she asked. He looked at her and all he could think was both, hard at first until the edge wore off, then it would be easy and leisurely. He shook off the sensual thoughts. *Stop* thinking with your dick. "Oh, babe, hard is my middle name," he said, his voice low and husky. It must have been a result of his downright dirty thoughts.

She took a quick breath and said, "Okay, we go right."

Once again, he was following her, her trailing light and flowery mixed with the sweet scent of woman as she sweated freely was as tantalizing as her. Damn but he liked the way she attacked the climb, sure-footed and confident. He wondered how she would fare at some more challenging climbs.

More spectacular views of the Hudson Valley and the river had him glancing to his left several times up the cliff, his focus fully on his progress as he enjoyed both the panoramic view, and the one above him. Just before the top, it got steep and he had to use all his concentration to navigate the outcropping. They emerged onto a flat area with more spectacular views over the river. She stood there her breathing even and deep. "That's Pollepel Island," she said pointing upriver, "and Bannerman's Castle, an abandoned military surplus warehouse." She turned to look at him. "Do you know much about the history?"

"No, not at all." He hadn't hiked here, in fact, he didn't know this trail even existed until he found the brochure near the elevator. Lately he was getting edgy and getting out of the city on day trips suited him. His choice would be something strenuous and sporty as he enjoyed the physical as much as the mental pursuits.

"The castle was built by Francis Bannerman who emigrated to the US in 1854 from Scotland. He opened a store on Broadway to outfit volunteers for the Spanish-American War and bought up most of the guns, ammunitions, and equipment captured by us. He built the castle when he found that his warehouse was too small. Then he built a smaller one as a residence. He died in 1918 and construction stopped. Unfortunately, there was an explosion that destroyed some of the warehouse portion and his home caught fire, too. There used to be tours, but when the ferry sank, the island pretty much was left vacant. There were tours later in the sixties, but a fire destroyed most of the structure and the tours ceased. It now belongs to New York State Parks and Rec as a historic site."

"That's an interesting story."

She smiled and nodded. He got a little lost in her eyes for a moment. They were so green. For what seemed like an eternity they stood there. She looked away first, reaching back for her pack and pulling out another bottle of water. She folded down to the ground and said, "There was a murder there, too. An engaged couple."

"He killed her?"

She shook her head with a wry cant to her mouth. His eyes inexplicably drawn there against his will. "She killed him."

His brows rose and he nodded. "Not usually how the story ends."

"Well, I hope when I'm engaged, I won't feel the need to do my fiancé in," she said with another one of those charming laughs.

"So you're single?"

"Yeah, in the dating pool. My friends, too. Seems it's hard to find a hot guy in the city."

He bit his tongue against asking her any more questions about her unattached status.

"How about you?"

"Casual dating." He shrugged. "My lifestyle is unconventional." He looked away wary of getting snagged by those green eyes again. But, he couldn't help wondering if that was a glint of disappointment in those verdant depths. He had to admit. He could make an exception with Callie, she intrigued him on so many levels, but it wouldn't be wise. He knew he would hurt her and she was much too sweet and down-to-earth to fit into his world. He wouldn't want to subject her to scrutiny of both the media and his "so-called" friends.

After their rest break and quick hydration, they were up again heading down a short declining dip, then a slight ascent through trees and meadow. After hiking for a bit, they reached a yellow marked trail which went to the right.

"I'm headed to the left," she said. "That's the Undercliff Trail and takes a bit longer, but I've got to get home to let Jack out, so I'm cutting it short today." She pointed off into the distance. "This way we can see Storm King Mountain across the river and Breakneck Ridge Trail is a loop, bringing us right back to the parking lot. We've gone less than a mile."

He raised his brows. "Seems longer than that."

"Lightweight," she said with a grin and then started on the white marked trail that rose steeply to a knob that delivered on the promise of another spectacular view.

"When there's white on Storm King Mountain, there's going to be rainfall later."

He looked at the view and something shifted in him, a release that made him take a deep breath. The Hudson was steeped with history from a busy waterway to the Revolutionary War when this whole area was contested between American forces and the British. The mountain rose up into the blue sky, from a smudged blue and gray to the variegated greens of the forests. He breathed deep, and even though he was a tried and true New York City native son, the freedom of this wide-open space freed that caged man and gave him a momentary respite. He could get used to this.

"It's an amazing feeling, isn't it?" Callie asked. She didn't elaborate and he realized that she was feeling the same way. Their silent communication setting off a desire to know this woman who seemed to be way more in tune with him than anyone he'd ever met. But he knew himself and the demands of his life were too much to overcome.

He turned away and they continued with the hike. The trail climbed, then leveled off and was much easier going than the rocky climb. They passed a great view of Sugarloaf Mountain, with a big bridge in the distance. Continuing their descent, they were careful to follow the trail markers and were rewarded with another view of Sugarloaf, but closer.

When they reached Route 9D they walked the worn path to the parking lot in the distance. He wanted to drag his feet and spend more time with her, but remembered not only was she off limits, but she lived next door.

He didn't want her to have any expectations, and he was quite aware that being friends with her would inevitably lead him right where he was trying to avoid going. She was too interesting, tantalizing, and sweet to resist.

When they reached the parking lot, she stopped and looked up at him from beneath her baseball cap, her green eyes sparkling from their hike and the fresh air. He wanted to ask her to meet him for coffee back in the city, but bit his tongue.

"Thanks for being my tour guide," he said instead, his desire to spend more time with her like a ball of jittering magpies in his gut. "See you around the homestead." He kept his tone casual when what he was feeling was anything but.

"Bye, Owen." She turned away and he couldn't stop himself from turning back around and watching her, regret pouring over him like a surprise downpour. "Not happening, McKay," he muttered. "Keep walking, buster."

Back in the city, he went into his loft wondering if she was already inside. As soon as he opened the door, he expected Jill to bound up and woof then come to him. But instead, she was lying on her doggie bed, her head on her paws.

He frowned and went over to her. "You sick, girl?"

Having this canine in his life was so strange. Before his great aunt died, he wasn't interested in having a pet. He didn't want the responsibility. Taking care of himself was all he could manage.

But she had been part of his aunt's life. She had loved Jill intensely, even though the young Great Dane wasn't with his aunt for very long.

Sorrow filled him, pushing out the benefits of that wonderful hike. He fondled the dog's head and cupped her under the chin. She blinked a few times and he was blindsided by the affection for her that came out of the blue.

He looked over at the clock on the mantle of his fireplace and realized he'd better get going. He had to walk her, feed her, and get to the club. He had some things he needed to do before they opened for the evening.

He stood up. "Come on, girl, let's get you outside. Maybe you'll feel better."

She didn't move right away, but when he reached for her leash, she pushed up. He frowned again at her lethargy. "Maybe you'll see that handsome Jack," he said and her tail started to wag.

He clipped the leash on and left his loft. At the elevator, he looked around, then realized he was searching for Callie. But she was MIA through Jill's walk and his return to his loft.

Even as he jumped in the shower, he couldn't seem to hide his disappointment even from himself. He was much to jaded to believe in happily ever after. His parents had been no kind of role models for him. In fact, they were nothing to him. He was alone in the world again, the brief time with his great aunt his only warm memories of his formative years.

He wasn't going to go soft here, not for a pair of gorgeous green eyes and something so sinfully sweet he would get a sugar rush. He was beyond true love and making a life with someone. His merry-go-round life wasn't conducive to marriage or children.

Cosmopolitan bachelor was etched in his cells, but as he dressed in lightweight black slacks, a gray mesh T-shirt and a deep purple jacket with satin lapels, he couldn't shake her from his thoughts.

Owen had a car service that picked him up every night from the curb outside his loft. As he came out of the building, he caught a glimpse of a shapely backside and a black and white Great Dane as they turned the corner. For a moment, he stood there, his impulse was to sprint after her.

"Sir?" the driver said.

He looked at the man blankly, then smiled and said, "Thanks," as he folded down into the black leather of the seats. He pulled up his expansion proposal on his tablet and made tweaks to it as the car threaded through the late afternoon traffic snarl, the driver waiting for throngs of people to cross.

Owen, immersed in his plan to get backing for a FLASH in LA, and Miami, kept getting disrupted by a sweet mouth and green eyes. He forced himself to stay on task until the car pulled up to his nightclub.

FLASH was located in West Chelsea in the meat packing district and had grown from a small one room location to a two-tiered multi-room nightclub with superstar DJs, spinning the latest in EDM—electronic dance music. Owen had gambled and with backers had opened a second FLASH in Vegas two years ago. That club opened with the highest-grossing profits for a club in the nation, with eighty-five million in revenue the first year.

Now he was getting noises from them, pushing for two more locations, the hip LA scene and the hot Miami beat. When he entered, his premiere bouncer, Axel Ruin was standing just inside the club. The guy was six-seven with a shaved head, packed muscle, and a deep voice with a tough accent of New York in it. He was actually just discovered by a LA casting agent who was interested in him for action/adventure movies. Ruin was down-to-earth, not a pretentious bone in his body. It would be interesting to see how that all panned out.

His floor manager, David Coates was already making the rounds and checking out every aspect of the club to make sure it was in pristine condition when it opened. He handled the wait staff as well as any disputes or minor problems on the floor. Ruin handled all the major ones.

"Hey boss," Ruin said as Owen passed.

"Good evening, Axel." Owen gave him a brief handshake before moving on. He waved to David who waved back. Heading to the back of the club where he kept his office, he unlocked the door and went inside and turned on the lights. He went behind his desk, set down his tablet, and removed his suit jacket, neatly hanging it on a metal rack to his right. Settling in his chair, he propped up his tablet and continued to work.

There was a knock at the door about thirty minutes later and Celeste Hearne, his controller and a seasoned nightlife office boss, came in. She was a stunning woman with dark eyes and hair and a curvy body. He'd dated her casually on and off. She wanted more, but he made it clear to her that their relationship was a mutual sex with the boss thing and that was it. She set down a stack of checks and they went through them.

"We have a bit of a problem with a remorseful spender."

"How much?"

"Five K and, Owen, he's a firefighter."

Owen sat back and said, "What happened?"

"Too much alcohol and too much partying. He came in with Terry Christian as a winner of a night on the town with a NBA player."

"Comp it," Owen said and started signing the checks. "

"Comp it? Five K?"

"Celeste. He's a first responder who probably was on top of the world to be partying with Christian. Comp the damn bill."

"Yes, sir."

"Don't call me sir."

"Yes, jerkwad."

He gave her a slight smile. "That's better. Make sure you let him know that we made a mistake. I don't want this to get out to the media."

"Yeah, you don't want any of those news mongers to know what a great guy you are."

"No, it'll ruin my rep. Now get out of here."

Three weeks later, Owen was kneeling beside Jill whose eating had been sporadic and she was still lethargic. He was worried about the damn animal, the guy who didn't want an ounce of responsibility. He really didn't have a vet, so he decided to take her to a clinic. Once inside he sat down with her. A little boy looked up at him. He had blond hair and an infectious grin. He eyed the dog that was bigger than him.

"You can pet her. She's really gentle." Owen smiled at the boy's mother who gave him an alarming look.

He reached out tentatively and stroked down the sleek, black Dane's back. Jill turned her head and licked him with a big, pink, very wet tongue. He giggled and went to stand behind his mother. Owen chuckled softly.

When his name was called, he led her into the examination room. The doctor came in and exchanged pleasantries with him. After her examination, the doctor looked at him and proclaimed the diagnosis. Owen's mouth dropped open and he just stared at the man. "You've got to be kidding?"

"There's no mistake, Mr. McKay."

31

Three weeks had passed since the impromptu hiking excursion with the delectable Owen McKay, and Callie was still telling herself she was relieved that he hadn't spoken to her or tried to ask her out. She knew her mind was strong, but her flesh was definitely still weak, even without renewed temptation. Just the memory of him spreading lotion over her back and shoulders gave her a sizzling quake down her spine and added to her fantasy storehouse.

But today when she got home from work, she found a note from Owen on her door. It said simply, "I need to talk to you."

Callie left Jack safely locked in the loft and walked across the hall to knock on Owen's door, determinedly ignoring the shiver of anticipation that coursed through her.

It seemed an eternity passed before he opened the door, but it was worth the wait. This time he was wearing only a pair of soft, faded jeans slung low on his hips and nothing else. His features were just as gorgeous as she remembered, but his lean jaw was clenched tight. His dark hair was a wet, disheveled, enticing mess around his head, making it clear that he'd only just ruffled it with a towel after stepping out of the shower. He looked so sinfully sexy he literally took her breath away. The dreams and fantasies of Owen that she'd spun over the past three weeks paled in comparison to the real thing.

He folded his arms across his broad, bare chest and leaned against the doorframe, his entire demeanor tense.

"We have a situation here."

"A situation?" Callie repeated, her heart starting to beat faster. Oh, God. Was he going to ask her out?

"Jack knocked Jill up."

Her expectations went thump. "Whaaaaat?"

"Jill's going to have puppies, and Jack's the only possible father."

CHAPTER THREE

"OH, MY GOD." Her dark green eyes widened, and he was struck by how expressive they were. "Are you sure?"

His dog was going to have puppies, but that wasn't the worst of it. He now was tied to this sweet, girl-next-door type he'd done his utmost to avoid. She didn't have the white picket fence, but she might as well have. Sharks like him swam in dark, murky waters, just waiting to gobble up a tasty morsel like Callie.

When he'd discovered that his dog was pregnant and realized that the culprit had to be Callie's Dane Jack, he'd thought about keeping mum. She wouldn't have known. But his conscience wouldn't let him. She had the right to know. But his problem was that Callie was too tempting and much too sweet for him. "Yes, I'm sure. There's no other way she could be pregnant."

He moved back and, just like an exotic scent on a restless wind, she followed him into his loft. He deliberately left the door open, as if that would protect her from him. "Were you planning to breed her?"

"No. I don't know anything about breeding a Great Dane, nor am I interested in doing it." Taking responsibility for Jill was more than he really wanted. But, he'd loved his great aunt Matilda. "My aunt didn't want me to be lonely." That had been the trouble with Matilda; her shrewd old eyes had missed very little.

"Then may I ask why she wasn't spayed?" Her earnest expression only made him want to reach out and do something naughty to change it. He dragged his hand through his hair, irritated with the whole situation. It was bad enough he had to be across the hall from all that temptation, now she had to become a part of his life. But it was futile to fight against it. "My great aunt had planned to breed her, apparently. She was a bit eccentric, but I loved her. She died five months ago and left the dog to me. I had no idea Jill hadn't been spayed. Turns out it's one of the reasons she is so unruly. Plus my great aunt indulged her shamelessly."

"I'm sorry about your great aunt. What was her name?" The words were obviously heartfelt, and her eyes conveyed her genuine sympathy. He was both touched and terrified by her completely open compassion, the sympathy in her eyes, and the soft cadence of her voice. Really, he should run like hell in the other direction rather than spend any more time with this woman.

"Matilda is...was her given name, but I always called her Aunt Tilly." He nodded, struggling against the sudden emotion that clogged his chest. That was the thing about grief. It snuck up on him when he wasn't looking or prepared.

"So, you must have had no clue that Jill was in heat."

He heard the jingle of Jill's collar tags and glanced down the spacious loft to see her emerge from his bedroom. She was a lean, lithe silhouette against the backdrop of New York and the setting sun. "No. But in retrospect, I can see that she'd been behaving differently."

Catching her gaze traveling over his chest, he suddenly wished he'd taken the time to throw on a shirt before he opened the door. She wet her lips and everything in him tightened. "Well, if it's any consolation, Jack is registered."

When her words penetrated his aroused brain, he groaned. "Oh, man. Now I feel like I've stolen a stud fee from you."

Callie laughed. "I wouldn't say that you stole it exactly, but Jack's sire and dam are champions, and my parents are the breeders. Jack-of-All-Trades is his sire and his dam is Pot of Gold. Jack's registered name is Lassiter Run's Jackpot."

He might be portrayed as a ruthless rogue of a nightclub owner in the *New York Scoop,* and he would agree that some of it was true, but most of the rag's stories about him were pure fantasy. But he wasn't a thief *anymore* and he certainly hadn't meant to breed his dog to Callie's. His thoughts returned to what she was saying and then it registered.

"Oh, crap. Jack-of-All-Trades? The champion Great Dane that has won more shows than any other Dane? Ha, great. Are your parents going to be angry?"

"How do you know about Jack's sire?"

"My great aunt. She followed all the dogs and their ranks. She loved to talk about it, especially at the end. I listened."

"They've been planning on putting Jack to stud, that's why he wasn't neutered. I don't know how they will take the news, but they'll be thrilled that he can perform."

Owen laughed and Callie smiled. His chest felt tight. Again.

"He's only two," she continued, "so my parents were waiting until he was a little older."

The only warning that he had before Jill sailed over the sofa like an Olympic-class hurdler was the jingle of her tags. She sprinted out the door and made a mad dash to Callie's door.

The dog's shoulder hit Callie, and she twisted away and landed with a thump on his dark mahogany floor as a whoosh exploded from her. She pushed herself up and snapped, "That dog is a menace."

"I'm sorry," he responded as he reached down and helped her up. Owen could hear Jack whining and pawing on the other side of Callie's door.

Jill snuffled along the edge of the threshold, pacing back and forth.

They walked into the hall and Owen grabbed Jill's collar. "This is a mess, but the worst part is that I'm freaked out about Jill."

Callie stopped in front of her door and said, "Quiet, Jack," but the crying continued. "What do you mean?"

"I have a pregnant dog. Does she need special food? Vitamins? What happens when she goes into labor? 'I don't know nothin' about birthing no puppies.'"

Callie laughed. "Calm down, Prissy," she said, continuing Owen's *Gone with the Wind* joke. "We'll fetch a doctor to help out."

"Ha ha."

Callie sobered. "Have you had her checked?"

"At a clinic, and I'm not taking her back there. I don't have a lot of confidence in their ability to handle my dog."

"Well, I have a friend who is doing her DVM residency at St. Mark's Veterinary Hospital. I'm sure she would make a house call."

Relief flooded him. "That would be great."

"She could recommend a vet from the hospital, too, because you'll want to take her for regular checkups during her pregnancy."

"I really appreciate your help with this." He looked away as he struggled to balance his desire to avoid getting close to this woman with the needs of his dog, and the sneaky, self-sabotaging inclinations of his traitorous body. Finally he decided it was better to take the plunge. "Would you be willing to provide Jill with some training?"

Initially, Callie looked wary. He couldn't really blame her, given that he hadn't exactly planned to ask until his mouth opened and the words popped out.

"Of course," she finally said and dug into her pocket, pulling out a business card.

Owen took the card, allowing his fingers to slide along hers. They tingled as she pulled her hand away.

And then he had to laugh immediately at her business name. "Sit Happens. Clever." Their chance bond was as unexpected as it was unwanted, and her adorable sense of humor only made the situation more difficult. At least for him.

"I have three girlfriends who are great at brainstorming. You should have heard some of the names they came up with. But a little humor is a good thing, and my business is thriving, as you'll see when you bring Jill in for her first lesson?"

"So you're Manhattan's dog whisperer?"

Callie chuckled.

"I'll make an appointment soon."

"Owen?"

He turned to find Celeste Hearne, standing at his elbow. He looked back at Callie and saw her eyes shutter as they traveled over the stunning woman. "Callie, this is Celeste."

Callie nodded at her in greeting. "I need to feed Jack. I'll see you tomorrow."

Owen wanted to tell her the truth. He wanted to tell her that Celeste was his financial manager, and whatever was between them was casual, but he kept quiet. It was better this way. Better she believed him to be the playboy the *Scoop* followed avidly. He wasn't into commitment, and Callie was the type of woman who would expect it. Owen knew that he'd only break her heart.

Owen gazed after her anyway as she slipped inside her loft, having to fight an agitated Jack, who gave her a very mournful doggie groan as she shut the door on his ladylove.

"I thought you went for the more…glamorous type, Owen." When he just gave her a stern look, she shrugged and continued. "I didn't mean to interrupt, but you wanted to go over the recent figures for the expansions, and I couldn't reach you on the phone."

"No, it's fine." He indicated she should precede him into the loft, dragging Jill with him and shutting the door. Jill eyed him, and then the door, and then him again with a very sad look on her face, but Owen ignored it. When she finally lay down in front of the door, he transferred his attention to Celeste.

As recently as last week, he'd thought of asking her out for dinner then sex, but now it didn't seem as appealing as it had been in the past. She understood the score, but now he felt uninterested for the first time in his life. Callie's lovely face and her heartfelt genuineness filled his imagination, and he shook his head abruptly. A part of him longed for that, but it just came with too many strings.

"Let's get to those numbers," he said, his voice rougher than he intended, as Celeste followed him into his home office.

The knock he was expecting on the door came late the next morning. Callie had been true to her word, and her friend Dr. Poe Madigan stood outside his door. She wasn't dressed as he expected a vet would be. She wore a black T-shirt with a skull on it, a short, plaid schoolgirl skirt, and black, thick-soled boots with buckles up the sides. She had very intelligent eyes that were both sensitive and warm, even though the blue-streaked hair threw him a bit.

"Hello," she said, but she was naturally dog-savvy and didn't even make eye contact with Jill.

Owen extended his hand and they shook. Jill sat down next to Owen and raised her paw. Poe laughed. "Looks like you've at least taught her that."

"Actually," he said, feeling a bit surprised, "my aunt must have taught her. I've never seen her do it."

"Well, dogs are pretty smart. I prefer them to humans."

He smiled and nodded, liking her blunt personality. "She likes to outsmart me."

Poe laughed again, and it was infectious.

"So, this is quite a predicament."

Owen nodded. "Yes, I'm just thankful Callie is being so…gracious." Thoughts of the girl next door should have been tame, but Owen had to shut down the track his mind was on. That one track would inevitably lead him to a complicated place, and he didn't want to go there.

Poe started a thorough and methodical examination of his dog, and he already felt better. Those twisting butterflies in his stomach over Jill's condition subsided some. Maybe he was developing a soft spot for her, which was something else that surprised him.

When Poe finished, she said, "She looks good. You take good care of her."

"Anything you can recommend?"

"Several things. Make sure she has a spacious whelping box. Get that together early, because she'll want to fuss with it. Her nesting instinct will be strong. Show her the area and let her explore it. Now, may I see what you're feeding her?"

He led her to the kitchen and pulled out Jill's dog food. "Oh, good stuff. I think that you can go ahead and keep feeding her this. It's packed with nutrients. I'm not an advocate of feeding her vitamins when the food she's receiving is top-notch. As the pregnancy progresses, you'll notice she'll be off her food now and again. If she goes two days without eating, make an appointment. Would you prefer I recommend someone from St. Mark's?"

"Aren't you a doctor?"

"Yes."

"A full-fledged one?"

"Yes. I'm doing my residency because I'm specializing in surgery, but I have my DVM from Cornell."

"Then I'd rather have you do Jill's checkups.

Poe smiled. "Okay. Here's my card."

Owen took it and tacked it to his fridge with a magnet.

"Toward the end of her pregnancy, you'll probably need to feed her more. I took the liberty of bringing our brochure with me that details the changes you can expect in your bitch. That should help."

"Thank you."

She nodded. "Well, I'll be off now."

"Hey, take this voucher for a night at my club. Bring your friends."

Poe looked down and her eyes widened. "I've always wondered about FLASH. I heard it's a rocking place."

"Darkwave? DJ Code Asylum?"

Her head came up. "I knew he'd been at your club, but the cover and the line with no chance of getting in was daunting. He's amazing, I love his cool blending of synth rock, darkwave music, especially electronic dance and downtempo."

Owen smiled. If it was one thing he knew, it was that people loved their music with a frenzy. "He was there and I'm sure I'll have him back. He's very popular and considered in the business to be very creative. Blending shoegazing—"

"Shoegazing? You are an interesting man, Owen McKay. Who thought you would know about guitar distortion, feedback, and obscured vocals." She waved her hand, her eyes glinting. "We could have a whole discussion on that alone." She bit her lip and reached for the vouchers. "All right. Thank you. I went to school to be a vet, and I swear I would do this job for free, so perks aren't really necessary."

"Your time is valuable, Poe, and for a nervous, expectant dog owner who's not completely comfortable with a dog, let alone a pregnant one, I'm grateful for you coming over here and giving me advice. It was nice of Callie to suggest it."

"Callie is wonderful and sweet." She narrowed her eyes. "And your rep says you're not. So don't make me put on my ass kicking boots."

He liked this girl's blunt, no nonsense way of communicating.

"I'm just her neighbor." He had every intention of remaining *just* her neighbor.

43

Her eyes said, *sure you are*. Poe waved a hand at him. "Thank you for the vouchers. Callie is a very good friend of mine. I'd do just about anything for her."

"Thank you for your kindness." She gave him another narrowed-eyed look. After she left, he went to get ready for work. "A whelping box," he murmured to himself. Jill's ears pricked and she gave him a mournful look. He'd have to figure out what the hell that was. "I think you've had enough of Jack for now, missy." This time she made a soft sound in her chest and he reached out and rubbed her silky head, affection hitting him square in the chest. "Puppies...yeesh."

The fact that she had been right about what type of woman Owen went for didn't make her feel any better. Wow, those gypsy eyes, and that perfect face, not to mention her dark, curly, just-out-of-bed hair and hot, slamming bod. Callie realized she didn't stand a chance against exotic-looking Celeste.

Wrong, wrong, wrong! She shouldn't be thinking about Owen at all. She stalked into the kitchen, feeling downright infuriated as she prepared Jack's dinner. He hadn't followed her in, so she suspected he was pouting. Well, let him pout. That female dog was freakin' out of control. The way she jumped over the couch like a gazelle was truly something to behold. But no dog owner should put up with that kind of behavior.

Unless. Callie wondered if she was a natural for agility training. Owen was athletic, with all his tight muscles that she worked hard not noticing—okay, she gave into her conscience, she noticed—so maybe that would be a good way, once the puppies were born for her to release some of that energy. He actually might enjoy bonding with Jill that way. She'd broach the subject and see what he thought.

"Are you hiding from me, mister?" Jack made another grunting noise and Callie couldn't help but smile. She was glad he couldn't see her. "You've got some 'splainin' to do, young man."

She pursed her lips and made rapid kissing noises as she set his bowl down. Jack came to the kitchen door and gave her a sheepish look. "Dinner," she said and pointed to the bowl. He walked over and sniffed it, and then looked at her with his expressive brown eyes and his adorable droopy lips.

"Nope, no Jill. You've done enough for now. Eat."

Jack let out a big sigh and settled down to his dinner.

Callie made her own dinner and sat at the table to enjoy her beautiful view of the city. She let her thoughts wander to when Jill had knocked her over and Owen had helped her up. She had felt his energy, and his heat. God help her, she was so attracted to that man. He had been visibly shaken by Jill's pregnancy, and it was clear that he only tolerated the dog because his beloved great aunt left her to him. The fact that he actually seemed to be interested in training and interacting with her melted Callie's heart. He was trying to be a good dog owner. Speaking of his great aunt, the fact that the old woman thought he was lonely piqued her interest. For heaven's sake, the man had a different woman every week. Why would anyone think he was lonely? She wanted to ask him that question. Maybe she would, caution be damned.

But it had been quite clear that he was indeed the bad boy described in the *Scoop*. She crunched on the croutons in her salad and let out as big a sigh as her poor, lovesick dog.

Callie checked Poe's harness and turned to look at her friend. They were at the climbing wall at Callie's gym and had spent about an hour getting Poe acclimated to climbing—tying knots, getting used to the automatic belay system, and getting a spot from below. She was upbeat and funny, entertaining people around her, but that was no surprise. It was quirky Poe at her best. "Why do I have to climb? I think it's for monkeys and those adorable sloths and koalas. They have the natural equipment. I'm in no way an ape."

Callie giggled and nudged Poe with her hip. "Because right now you're the only one who knows about...*it*." Just when she thought she had everything under control, that's when it all went to hell. Yeah, she'd gotten tangled up with Owen, he'd fallen on her and she'd gotten lost in the fantasy, but she was whistling Dixie if she thought things could work out between them. Regardless of the mess their dogs were in, they could be adults about it. She bit her lip. She needed to tell her parents. That would have to become a priority.

Poe looked right and left and lowered her voice. "It? What are we talking about here?"

Callie loved her adorable, weird, sometimes totally clueless friend. "The puppy pregnancy." Jack was going to be a daddy and that was unexpected. He was still a bit young, but it was obvious he had what it took. Her parents would be happy about that. It was a good selling point. Obviously, part of this fiasco was her fault.

"Oh, right," Poe said checking her harness again, releasing a quick laugh. She looked over at Callie. "Owen's hot by the way and his Great Dane is freaking adorable." She was dressed in her usual way, even for climbing, in a pair of stretchy black leggings with pentagrams on them and a tank top with a large cross on the front, the center of it decorated with a skelly and the racer back small, black mesh roses. Callie was in something plain.

"Yes, now you can see what I'm up against."

Callie put her hand in the middle of Poe's back, propelling her forward as the two men who were spotting them got set with the ropes. There was definitely resistance. "Hand over hand," Callie said. "Make sure your feet are secure before you move up."

She nodded and took a breath, tucking a stray hair behind her ear. "I totally get it. He's got a killer smile, hot bod, beautiful blue eyes."

Callie was trying to forget those wonderful assets. "Stop cataloging him." Poe looked up with a pensive expression. "I know all those things. You're stalling."

Poe looked at Callie again with one of her winsome smiles that probably got her out of most things and, Callie bet it especially worked on the opposite sex. "I guess this would be a really bad time to tell you I'm afraid of heights."

"No, you're not. You're just lazy."

She huffed a breath. "I'm not lazy. I have a healthy sense of self-preservation and being aware of my strengths and weaknesses." Callie gave her a sidelong, you're-not-fooling-me look. "Okay, I'm basically lazy."

"Climb, smarty pants. Expand your horizons. Just think. When the Zombie Apocalypse comes, you'll be able to outclimb them."

Her face scrunched up and she laughed and shoved Callie's shoulder. "Zombies don't climb."

The guy behind them said, "Maybe stairs, but that's stretching it."

Poe turned around and gave him a brilliant smile, and the poor guy didn't have a chance. "Very perceptive. You a Zombie expert?"

He said, "Love the movies."

"Hey how about—"

"You stop flirting and start climbing. We're going to run out of time," Callie said giving the guy a stern look. He shrugged his shoulders. Couldn't blame the guy for trying to make time with Poe, she was a trip. "How about we go back to the concept that we're expanding your horizons."

Poe stuck out her bottom lip. "Did anyone ever tell you you're pushy?" she asked with a grin.

"Get going, sweetie pie."

"I'm no ape," Poe muttered under her breath but put her foot on the first toehold and started up. "But I'm going to work on channeling one." Callie, couldn't help but laugh. The two guys behind them were thoroughly entertained. Both of them were pretty cute, too. She glanced over then down. "Ooh, this is high."

"Just don't look down and you'll be fine." Callie, grabbed for a handhold and pulled herself up. Poe was moving pretty easily as she made a soft grunting noise on the next push.

"Can I ask you a question?" she asked, her concentration centered on her climbing.

"Of course." Callie moved sideways to get a better vantage point.

"Do you like Owen?" Poe asked, her tone of voice casual, but the question felt as if she'd hit Callie with a sledgehammer.

"Define like," she said.

"Now who's stalling for time?" She was a perceptive little dickens, Callie thought. Answering questions about Owen was not something she really wanted to do, but she needed to be honest with herself. That's what Poe's question did, made her

48

think about it. Poe increased the pace and Callie realized that this girl had a natural ability for this. With her comments about fitness being much too much work, Callie figured she'd been weak, but not the case. "Would you like to get to know him, if you didn't know about all that celebrity stuff. Just him one on one?"

Callie was surprised by her answer. "Yes, I think I would. He's funny, sweet, a good conversationalist, flirty."

"Maybe you should cut him some slack. Usually what's printed, especially in the *Scoop*, is a bunch of exaggerations and lies to drum up drama." She actually made it to the top before Callie." She yelled, "I am an ape and started making ape noises. Callie almost lost her grip.

When she came abreast of her, she said, "Here I thought you weren't even going to get halfway."

"I do yoga."

"You said you hate to exercise."

"Yoga isn't exercise, silly. It's a way of life." After that she pushed off the wall and shouted "Geronimo," as she repelled down.

Callie shook her head and followed her, shouting, "Geronimo," too.

The Zombie guy asked Poe for her number and the second guy asked for Callie's. His name was Charlie and he was a dental student at NYU. She gave it to him and later on that evening, she met the girls for cocktails. Poe told them all about the experience, her eyes glowing.

"Have you had any more run ins with Mr. Gorgeous?"

Brooke frowned. "It must be so hard to live next door to him and keep your mind off him."

"It's going to be even more difficult to do that now."

"Why?"

"Jack got Jill pregnant."

For a moment there was complete silence, then everyone of them burst into laughter. Callie looked up to the ceiling for divine help. "I'm glad you all think that's hilarious."

"Oh my God," Harper said, wiping at her eyes. She raised her hand. "Champagne over here."

"What are we celebrating?"

"The biggest laugh we've had in a long time," Brooke said. "Jack is so darn cute, Mr. Gorgeously stud."

Callie laughed despite her turmoil over having to deal with Owen. "Stop it."

"I can't help it. He's such a big, sweet, lovable lug." Then she sobered. "I so don't want you to get hurt, though, so be careful."

She touched Brooke's arm, and her friend's face and eyes softened. "It'll be fine. Nothing's changed except a few dozen little bundles of fur."

"We should go to his club," Harper said with a mischievous smile.

"That's an exclusive club and a tough door. The line will be endless," Brooke said, downing a quarter of her martini.

"I've got vouchers he gave me, so we can get in," Poe said.

"I don't need no stinking voucher," Harper laughed. "I'm a regular there, and I know the doorman."

"Of course she does," Poe murmured and rolled her eyes. "She knows practically everyone. It's too pricey for me."

"Don't worry, with Callie, we'll get the VIP treatment. We're just going to meet Owen, and I'm sure he'll be generous with the drinks."

"I don't know—"

"Come on. It'll be fun," Harper said. Brooke looked worried and Poe resigned.

CHAPTER FOUR

THE NEXT DAY, Callie said, "Don't laugh. It's not funny."

"It most certainly is funny," Brooke said as she cleaned Jack's ears. They were in one of Brooke's grooming rooms at Pawlish, her pet grooming service in the Lower East Side. She cupped Jack's face and pursed her lips. "He's a big stud-muffin," she said in a cutesy baby voice. Jack made a deep rumbling noise in his chest, and Brooke burst into laughter again. "He's a big, lovable, studly stud-muffin."

"Stop it," Callie said, but she, too, couldn't contain her mirth, and rubbed Jack's head affectionately. "Don't encourage him. He's in enough trouble."

"What did your parents say?" Brooke asked with another chuckle.

She tried to keep from flinching at that. "I haven't told them yet. I just heard and I really think they'll take it well, but I'll call my mom or maybe even go out there."

"You know she will be understanding. It was, after all, an accident. I adore your mom." Brooke frowned.

"I think once they see Jill, they'll be okay with it. It's not like Owen tried to steal Jack's…ah…pedigree."

Brooke snickered. "No, he obviously is clueless about females."

"Female dogs, anyway. He's not clueless about females at all."

Brooke took a brush from the grooming counter and paused. "Oh, no. What happened?"

"Just a stunning gypsy goddess, who showed up when we were talking in the hall after Jill soared over the sofa like an Olympic hurdler in an attempt to get to her stud-muffin." Jack's ear pricked at the mention of Jill's name.

"You sound jealous and miffed. I thought you were going to steer clear of this guy. I don't want to see you hurt."

"I was, then Jack had his way with Jill, and—lo and behold— we're connected by puppies."

Brooke gave her a sidelong glance, her eyes sparkling as she efficiently whisked the brush through Jack's glossy coat.

"I *will*," Callie insisted. "Stay away from him, I mean."

"Uh huh.

"Stop being your skeptical self for one minute. I promise to think of your stern look every time I feel any attraction to Owen. That should kill it stone dead."

Brooke raised a brow.

"Does that make you feel better?"

She set the brush down and kissed Jack on the bridge of his black and white nose. "Marginally. But, seriously, Callie. Is he the guy for you or someone to spend time with? I guess if you wanted a fling and could handle it, then that's a different story."

"Yes, I know, Owen is exciting and handsome."

"Right, but that's not everything."

It was Callie's turn to give Brooke the sidelong glance.

Brooke smiled and nodded. "Okay, it's something. I'm not immune. I've seen his picture and he's gorgeous, slick, and very public. Which, by the way, you're not—public, I mean. You want to be more practical. We're not exactly young, hip city girls anymore."

"I'm not sure I ever was, but I see your point. I'm so not glamorous and the women he pals around with are always dressed to the nines. I'm not sure I fit into that world. I'm comfortable with who I am and don't really want to change."

"Callie, I believe you could fit in any world you choose, but it's a matter of losing your heart and getting hurt by someone who can't commit. That's all."

"Mature business owners like us have to be smart. It's pretty clear that Owen is commitment-phobic."

"There you go. Good for the sprint, but lousy for the long haul." Brooke glanced at her watch. "Do you have time for lunch?"

"I would, but I'm meeting the guys for some basketball. Connor had to go overseas for a medical conference, so they're a man down."

"Okay. Then how about you all come over to my place for lunch after our dog park meeting."

"That sounds great."

"You want me to hold onto Jack? He so loves being here and he's never a problem. I can have Rachel watch him until you're done."

"That would be excellent. The community center's in the opposite direction and Ian's call was short-notice."

"No problem. I'll watch Mr. Gorgeously stud-muffin," she said and Jack woofed and made that wonderful rumble in his chest like he was agreeing about his prowess. Callie laughed.

She left Pawlish and headed down the street on foot since she loved walking and it wasn't far. The walk would warm her up nicely to whoop their butts.

She entered the community center and made for her locker where she kept her basketball clothes. She took off her street wear, and donned a pair of black Lycra shorts, a gray T-shirt with her name and logo on it, socks, and basketball high tops. She pulled her long hair back, then braided it to keep it out of her way.

She left the locker room and went down the hall. An arm snaked around her neck and a deep, voice, slightly accented with New York, said, "What's a babe like you doing in a sketchy joint like this?"

She laughed and turned to find Jesse Malone. One of Ian's best friends and partners at AlphaGroup, he had movie star features, the combination of black hair and stunning blue eyes kept him on the New York woman's radar even after his New York Five hockey days were behind him. Nicknamed Fast and Furious, he never slowed down and now in his mid-thirties, he still was hard and muscular. He wrote sports for the *New York Times* and commentated on games during the NHL season.

They entered the gymnasium. "Hanging out with these old scrubs."

"Who you calling old?" Her bother Ian and Calder West, another one of Ian's friends asked in unison.

They looked at each other and then laughed and bumped knuckles.

"Thanks for filling in, sweetheart," Calder said as he bussed her cheek. "The only problem is you and Ian will probably beat our asses and I hate losing…at anything."

"Competitive asshole," Jesse said.

Callie laughed. "Get ready to lose to a *girl*."

"Did you say, girls?" Jesse said, stealing the ball from Ian and ran off to their court, laughing.

Ian looked at Callie and there was a glint of retribution in his dark brown eyes. "Let's go kick their asses," he said.

Ian and Callie were a powerhouse pair. She grew up playing with him in back of their parents' house. Their father had installed the basketball hoop to teach Ian coordination and to get him out of the house and away from both video games and drawing. He hadn't grown out of either. But their dad couldn't complain. Her brother had really been quite a success in his life. He hooked up with Calder, Jesse, and Connor in college and they had not only been the best of friends and still were, but they had built the lofts she was living in and then with Calder's keen mind for finance, they were set when graduating from college. Calder, ever mindful of giving back to the community and helping those less fortunate than him, he'd started AlphaGroup as both a profit-making venture and a foundation to support people who made application.

She and Ian won four out of six games, all of them drenched by the end, some with sore elbows from hitting the deck, others a couple of bruises here and there. When they all hit the locker rooms, Callie hit the showers. As she was drying off, she was dismayed at how comfortable she felt here on the court, but couldn't figure out how to glam up for one of Harper's fundraisers. She was a hopeless tomboy mess.

Dressed in her street clothes, her athletic stuff now in a bag to be brought home and washed, she met the guys coming out of the locker room. All of them were dressed impeccably looking like ads for Old Navy and Banana Republic.

"Wow, you old scrubs clean up nicely."

"Right back at you," Calder said.

"Drinks and dinner?" Jesse suggested, but Callie was already shaking her head.

"I can't. I left Jack with Brooke—"

"Call her," Ian suggested. "Come on, we haven't seen you in a while. Jack will be fine."

She really wanted to go. It was fun to interact with Ian's friends who never made her feel like she didn't fit into this upscale group. She debated on whether or not to tell Ian about Jack getting Owen's bitch pregnant, but then decided against it. He couldn't keep his mouth shut and would spill the beans to their parents, even if he said he wouldn't.

"I not really dressed for it."

"You look great," Calder said. "I agree with Ian. Come with us."

She lost her resolve because she had a soft spot for Calder. "All right. Let me call Brooke, and she if she will dog sit my big man."

She pulled out her cell and pressed Brooke's number. "Hello, how was the game?"

"Great. Ian and I won the majority of the matches."

"Yeah, Sugar Ray Callie!"

"That's actually a boxing reference, but I'll take it."

Brooke laughed. "Mr. Gorgeous-muffin is sleeping right now. He exhausted himself frolicking with the other dogs."

"Really? Aw, poor tired boy." Callie laughed softly. "I was wondering if you wouldn't mind watching him for a few hours. The guys want me to go out to dinner with them."

"Of course. Go. I'll take Jack home with me. Roscoe will be happy to have a playmate for the evening. I'll feed him, so don't worry."

"You are the best. Thanks, Brooke."

They went to one of the oldest uptown bars in the city, Liberty Tavern which was in a historical building. Once inside, the hostess recognized Jesse right away and they were seated in the back near the bar.

Callie settled between Ian and Calder, and they ordered drinks.

The conversation flowed around Callie's business, Ian's art and upcoming gallery show, and segued into their love lives.

"How's Linda?" Callie asked. She hadn't seen Jesse with his wife in a long time. She had been a rink bunny he'd married. She was a bit flighty and high-strung, but seemed deeply in love with Jesse.

Jesse said, "We're getting a divorce." He sat back, his jaw hardening. "She's never been able to get over my celebrity and her jealousy destroyed us. I couldn't handle her mistrust anymore. We've done nothing but fight and argue for the duration of our marriage."

Callie said, "I'm sorry, Jesse." The other guys looked sympathetic, but like they'd rather be chewing nails then getting into emotion-laden topics. "I hear that you're going to be doing fan night with the Fives when the season starts up. The kids will love that."

"Hey, mates," a posh British tinged voice said and all of them swiveled in their chair to see Connor wending his way through the tables and chairs. His dark, close-cropped afro a mass as of curls reflected the light, his dark skin burnished in the glow. Callie jumped up when he reached the table and hugged him. "How's me stand in, love?"

"I'm great. It's so good to see you. When did you get back?"

"Just about an hour ago. I had enough of the conference and wanted to get back home. It's good to see you too, poppet."

He shook hands with his friends and settled into a chair that Jesse pulled from a vacant table.

All of them seemed to be relieved to move on from Jesse's sad news, but Ian gave her a sly grin. "Oh, we're not going to let you off the hook or move past your love life. What do you have to hide?"

At that exact moment, Callie looked toward the bar and slammed right into the dark blue eyes of Owen McKay. He lifted his glass to her. She was riveted to her seat, his eyes going over her in a sensual slide of slow seduction. She couldn't seem to get anything past her now tight throat, butterflies exploding in her tummy.

"Excuse me for a minute." She rose, setting her napkin on the table and walked toward him. "Are you stalking me?" she asked.

He smiled, "We do seem to be in the same place at the same time, like it's cosmic fate."

She chuckled. "It's a small world, even in Manhattan."

"I'd offer to buy you a drink, since we have puppies to celebrate and we are the proud puppy parents, but it looks like you're busy."

"Yes, I'm here with my brother."

"I recognized him. I also recognize Jesse Malone. He's been in the club a few times."

"The other men are Calder West and Dr. Connor Wentworth, he's a well-known reconstructive surgeon."

"Ah, West the financial genius. I've heard of him. But don't know the good doctor. Luckily I haven't needed his services."

"I'd better get back," she said, unable to take her eyes off him. He reached out and snagged her hand, kissing the back of it.

"See you around the homestead." He held her tightly for a moment, then let her go.

When she got back to the table, her brother eyed her with speculative and worried eyes. She was sure her cheeks were flushed, but thanked the dim lighting in here to hopefully mask it.

"What was that?" Ian asked leaning his elbows on the table, his overprotective brother instincts on full alert. "Was he hitting on you?"

"Ian, he lives next door. We are acquainted."

Calder also sat forward, and now she was bracketed with walls of muscle and overprotective males on either side. "He's a notorious playboy, Callie."

She turned to look at Calder who had the same look on his face, and now, geez, so did Jesse. "Want me to have a talk with him?" Jesse asked. His New York accent a little thicker when he got riled up.

"No, *Dad*, thanks. I can handle Owen McKay."

Ian touched her arm. "Seriously, Callie. I know you. He's a bad boy in just about anyone's book. You can't tame him or change him. I should know. Steer clear."

She rolled her eyes. "Ian, I can take care of myself and I've sworn off bad boys. Then she pierced Jesse, Connor and Calder with laser looks. "Except you three."

"I'm all for free love," Connor said, smiling. "No scolding from me."

He laughed and that broke the tension for the most part. When she looked over at the bar again, Celeste was sitting next to him and they looked pretty cozy. Well, Ian did warn her, the *Scoop* was pretty clear about their message and if that wasn't enough, Brooke's disapproval would be legendary. She pulled her eyes away from him as Calder won the bill grab between the men. Callie was happy to have them pay keeping their fragile macho male egos intact.

As they were leaving, she stood outside saying goodbye to her brother, Connor and Jesse as they shared a cab.

"How about you? Want to share a cab?" Calder asked.

"You're going in the opposite direction. Don't tell me I'm going to get a lecture. I already have a mom."

He chuckled and slipped her arm through his. "Okay we'll walk for a bit, but you're not going to get out of the lecture."

She sighed heavily. "I'm not involved with him."

"I think you are, sweetie. There's no mistaking that kind of look."

"I didn't say anything because Ian will blab to my parents, but Jack got Jill pregnant."

Calder chuckled and said, "Jack shall have Jill; Naught shall go ill."

"Shakespeare got it wrong. This was a terrible accident."

"Not on the dogs' part, I think."

She laughed, and said between bursts. "It's not funny." Slapping him on his shoulder.

He flashed her a grin. "If you say so."

"I do." She laughed again. "Brooke called him a studly stud-muffin."

"Yeah, that dog has the chops."

She burst into laughter again as they turned down a block, the wind picking up a bit. She could see the moon above her as her head went back.

They laughed for a few minutes. Then she sobered. "I have no idea what my parents are going to say."

"I don't envy you that." He was still chuckling.

"Don't tell blabbermouth."

He zipped his lips. "Mum's the word. "Now about Owen McKay—"

"There's nothing to worry about."

He gave her a stern look.

"I'm so not his type."

"I think female is his type."

"No, you're wrong. He likes the glamour girls, ones that look like they stepped out of a magazine fully coifed. I don't have that kind of look. I'm beer not champagne."

He stopped dead and she stumbled a bit. Whirling on her, he grabbed her shoulders and said with a growl, "You are not beer. You're beautiful, talented and if he can't see that, he's a complete fool! I think I'm going back there and punch his lights out."

As he headed back toward the tavern, she chased him down and grabbed his arm. "Calder, no. You'll get arrested and get thrown in jail. It's not worth it."

"Oh yes, it is. You're Ian's little sister." He swallowed and she looked up into his blue eyes and her heart did a little jump. *Oh, that was it.* She didn't embarrass him by saying anything or make him feel any worse than he was already probably feeling. For her, Calder had been like a big brother all her life. But it was clear it wasn't how he felt about her. She decided then and there she would never bring it up, but Calder, being the man he was would never jeopardize his friendship with Ian to pursue his little sister.

She guessed all the clues were there, but she'd been blind. She hugged him around the waist, and he hugged her back. They stood like that for a few minutes as traffic passed and cabs honked, lights changed from green to red and back.

"I'll always be here for you, Callie. No matter what. Just say the word."

"I know," she murmured.

After that, she insisted on him getting a cab for her, then heading home. When she got to Brooke's to pick up Jack, she asked, "Did you have a good time?"

"Sorta."

"Why? What happened?"

"Owen McKay was at the bar and he was with that stunning woman who Callie had seen at his place."

"Sure, they've had an on again/off again relationship. Was it hard to see them all lovey dovey?"

She petted Jack's head, settling him down. "Yes. Am I pathetic?" she couldn't keep the disappointment out of her voice.

"No, you're adorable and wonderful." Brooke said, slinging her arm around Callie. "Come on. I've got rocky road ice cream. Your favorite." She smiled and went with Brooke into the kitchen. Ice cream wouldn't take the edge off, but she went anyway.

After she got home, she locked the door behind her and wondered if Owen was in his loft with Celeste right now, her hands all over him. She went into her room to change into her pajamas, then paused and looked at herself in the full-length mirror. Most women had some problem with their body. But Callie really liked hers. She kept fit from walking a lot during the day, and staying active. She wondered if Owen thought about her like she thought about him. According to Calder, his type was female, but she was sure he was wrong.

She closed her eyes and groaned softly. She was driving herself crazy over this man and it had to stop. She started to grab a T-shirt out of her drawer, then stopped and reached for her frilly drawer. Snagging a tank top and shorts with lace on them, she pulled them on, then looked at herself again. She looked pretty good in girly stuff, even with her athletic body. With a smile, she went into the bathroom to brush her teeth.

The next day she was just walking into Sit Happens, when her cell rang. The display told her that it was her mom and it was time Callie told her about Jack's accident.

"Mom, are you in the city?"

"No, not yet, but I will be in an hour. How about meeting me for lunch?"

"Is Dad coming?"

"No, he can't we have several bitches that are going to whelp any day and that old worry wort won't leave them even for a short excursion. I happen to have an appointment with possible adopters and want to talk to them before we turn a puppy over to them, you know, see the layout of their place."

Callie bit her lip. Her mom was so meticulous about who adopted one of their Great Danes, Callie wasn't sure how she was going to react when she found out Jack had mated with a dog she hadn't approved.

"That sounds great. I need to talk to you anyway."

"Is everything okay?"

"Yeah, nothing horrible. I'll see you at our usual place at noon."

She saw her mom waiting outside for her. Her mom also looked good. She used to have sandy hair the same color as Callie's, now she covered the gray with a rinse. Her eyes were the same green and she had an infectious smile and trim body. She also loved working outside. They hugged and went inside and were seated immediately.

"How's things?" her mom asked, picking up the menu.

"Going well. I got several new clients and am really busy."

"Very nice." She looked over the menu for a moment, then set it down. "Your dad's talking about taking a trip again. Wants to hold off on any more breeding. Says we deserve one. I swear, that man."

"You both work hard. You do deserve to get away. I could take a week away from work to handle the kennel if you'd like."

She reached across the table. "You and your brother. We sure did something right there."

"He offered, too?"

"Yes."

"The suck up."

Her mother laughed. "He says he can paint outside and likes the idea of getting away from the city for a week. I know it's more difficult for you, so let him do it."

"Only if I get a peach cobbler, too."

Her mom looked innocent.

"Yeah, you're going to make him a pile of food before you go. I want my cobbler, too."

"All right. I'll make two cobblers, but you'll have to come out when they're done because you know you can't trust your brother."

They both laughed. "When and where are you going?"

"To Florence. We've always wanted to see it. It's a tour. We do love enjoying other people's company. You know how your father loves to jabber."

Callie smiled indulgently. Both her parents were such social people and though it was true her dad was a talker, her mom kept right up with him. "I brought the brochure so you can look at it."

Callie gave the waitress her order and waited until her mom had, too, then leaned back as the girl left. She decided it probably wasn't the best time to break the news. She should just wait and take Owen out there. The way her mom was, she'd want to see the dog as soon as possible. Callie couldn't make the trip until this weekend and making her mom wait would be agony for her. "Let's see that brochure."

"Is something wrong?" Her mom was in a great mood, but she was preoccupied with her dad's attempts to get away from the kennel. She didn't want to burden her right now with more puppies.

"No, nothing important. So, what are you up to this Saturday? Besides planning a trip?"

"Nothing out of the usual. Did you want to come by and have dinner? Your father would love that."

"Yeah, that sounds great. I haven't seen Dad in at least a month. He must be having daughter withdrawal."

Her mom laughed softly. "You know him two well. Sometimes he stands by your picture. He picks it up and sighs, then puts it down and sighs. Sounds like he's at his limit."

"He is so sweet."

"Don't I know it. He's the love of my life. I don't know what I would do without him. I can only hope you and your brother find that kind of person. I despair at getting any grandchildren out of Ian, but I have hope with you." She smiled and reached across the table grasping Callie's hand.

"Aw, Mom, I hope so, too," Callie said, and then couldn't help but think about Owen and wondered if they were able to get past all this bull, maybe they would have a chance. But she didn't want a chance. She wanted a sure thing, and he wasn't interested in committing. She would be setting herself up for heartache.

The food came to the table and Callie started to eat. She got butterflies all over again at the thought of him seeing her hometown, meeting her parents, and seeing the kennel. It was all so bucolic and far from his scene, but she couldn't help getting excited at the thought of spending a day with him, even though she shouldn't have.

CHAPTER FIVE

OWEN STOOD at his window and watched the sun rise. Celeste was behind him in his bed. Even as she stirred, he felt nothing but impatience. He realized that he might have had a nice time with this woman, the matter complicated by the fact that they worked together, but for him, it was over. Sating his physical needs and hers was all that he was going to be capable of doing. In fact, this *physical* thing was getting old.

Not true. Your physical reaction to Callie Lassiter was quite real last night.

Maybe that was why he'd ended up in bed with Celeste. To prove to himself he could just resume his life and not take the sweet dog whisperer into consideration at all. As if he hadn't met her. But he had and they were now connected by this puppy thing.

Maybe he was doing it for the publicity and that made him sick to think about it. He'd garnered attention early in his nightclub days, but that was about keeping himself footloose and fancy free and his personal life to himself.

"Owen, come back."

He turned to find her looking like a fashion model with her long curly hair dark against his light blue sheets. Her perfect features scrunched in impatience.

"I'm going for a run. Feel free to use the shower and have some breakfast. Make sure to lock up after you're gone."

She sat up. "What? Don't you want to eat with me?"

He sighed and then sat down on the bed. She smiled and reached for him, but he intercepted her hand and clasped it, keeping it from touching him. Her face fell when she focused on his, and she snatched her hand away. "We're going to have the talk, again."

"No, not exactly. Look, we have had a good time, and I was drunk last night. We both were. I think we should relegate our relationship back to a professional one."

Her jaw bunched, and she stared at her hands for a moment, then took a big breath. "I was thinking the same thing. You're not really here anymore when we're together. Who is she?"

"There isn't anyone," he said looking away.

"Bullshit, Owen." She threw back the covers and started to pull on her clothes. "Don't lie to me. I know you're preoccupied with another woman. Fashion model? Celebrity? Fortune 500 CEO? Who?"

"She's not famous," he said under his breath, thinking that Callie was more interesting to him than any of those high-powered people.

Her eyes narrowed. Then she laughed. "That girl next door? The dog trainer? Really, Owen."

"I'm not getting involved with Callie," he said anger curling through him, aggravated that she was acting so possessive when they were mostly friends with benefits. "Don't get so wound up. I've never made any damn promises to you, Celeste. I made that completely clear," he ground out through clenched teeth. "This is about my dog. Jill is pregnant by her Great Dane and we have to interact, but I wouldn't subject her to my world. She's much too sweet for that."

She tucked in her shirt and grabbed up her boots. "If you say so."

"Celeste?" he said before she exited. "Are we okay? I don't want our working relationship to be awkward or uncomfortable."

"In other words, if it is, I need to find other employment?"

"Is it? Do you want to leave?"

"No and no. I love working for you. It won't be awkward."

"Good. I'll see you tonight then."

"Okay. Bye."

She left the room, and Owen couldn't shake the sense that Celeste wasn't all right with the situation. He really didn't want to deal with a woman and her hidden machinations, especially with this expansion on the horizon and new backers to keep happy. He'd keep an eye on her.

He had his run and puttered around his loft. Jill was a little livelier, but she was still a bit off her food. He'd call Poe if it didn't pick up soon. Damn, Poe made him think of Callie and thinking about Callie made him want to see her. At five, he dressed for the club, a gray/blue hoodie beneath a blue jacquard jacket and slim black trousers. He fed Jill and was happy to see that she ate her whole meal. He petted her and said, "Good girl." She looked up at him with an expectant face. "Nope. You had your long walk today. You were lagging and if you're thinking about that guy across the hall, you need to rethink it. You're in enough trouble."

She made a mournful sound and his heart softened a bit. Damn dog. "Okay, maybe later. But for now, I have to get to work and keep you in kibble."

He exited the loft and every day since he'd "met" Callie, he found himself looking for her expectantly. But he got down to the lobby without any sightings, not even one in the street. He went right to his car waiting at the curb and got inside. He wasn't disappointed, he told himself. He had no expectations where Callie was concerned. *So, why can't you get her off your mind?*

As soon as he hit the club, it was nonstop action. At about nine, he left his office to do laps. This was the hand shaking, be seen time and interact with the people. The DJ was spinning Ambient music, a tonal and atmospheric structure and rhythm on the stage and the music was loud. Lights were flashing and the place was packed. He went to the door. "Ruin?"

"Yes, sir."

"Are we over our count? I don't want the fire marshal in here closing us down."

"No, sir, just at capacity. I'm keeping it all up here." He tapped his forehead.

Then he saw them. He recognized Harper Sinclair right away. There was no mistaking Manhattan's Darling. She was decked out as usual. Then Poe, wearing something off the wall that was studded black leather sexy, another woman who he didn't recognize, but was also stunning, then, he took a breath. Callie.

She was dressed in a hot pink scuba dress that hugged every inch of her delectable body. Her hair was in a mass of curls, makeup subtle and she carried a small glittering bag. He couldn't take his eyes off her. He was struck dumb.

As the four women approached the door, bypassing the line that snaked around the block, Harper said, "Ruin, my man. Entre' please."

Ruin held up his hand. "Ah, it pains me to say this, ladies. We're—"

He found his voice. "Let them in," Owen said and Ruin knew when he meant business. He didn't say a word, unclipped the velvet rope and let them file in one at a time, then he clipped it back on.

Owen watched Callie as she passed, Harper giving him one of her overprotective chick looks. He leaned over and said, "Get four people out. Start moving the door a bit, get some circulation. Start with people who have been here the longest."

"But that's Tango's group. He's got like twelve partiers and they have a table."

Tango was an A-list music rapper. "Offer them free drinks the next time they come in. Better yet, tell him I want to talk to him about spinning."

"Yes, sir. He'll eat that up with his ego."

Owen nodded and then turned to look for the four women. They were at the bar and Owen came up behind them. He flagged the bartender. "These ladies drink for free."

He nodded and slid their money back to them.

Harper grabbed up her cocktail and turned to him. "Just as smooth as ever, Owen."

"And, you're just as beautiful as ever, Harper."

She laughed softly, but then her eyes flashed. Owen had meant every word, and she couldn't find the lie in him because it wasn't there. There had been a time when he and Harper had been close to getting intimate, but Harper came with a high-maintenance tag, a demanding sassy personality, and commitment written all over her. So, why-oh-why couldn't he apply the same common sense to Callie?

"Thanks for the vouchers," Poe said. "Callie wanted to stay home but we made her come. She's such a homebody."

"Poe," the unknown woman said, nudging her and Callie looked up to the ceiling.

Owen was so damned charmed, he laughed.

"We haven't met," Owen said, extending his hand and the pretty brunette, determined not to be charmed took it was a quick, efficient shake. "Brooke Palmer." He liked her librarian look and censuring gaze. She was stoically in Callie's camp.

"I'm not much of a party girl. Had to be frugal with my money." She smiled sweetly.

"In other words, my drinks are overpriced?"

She shrugged.

"Brooke," Callie said, her brows raised, her eyes telling Brooke she was being backhanded rude. Owen wasn't usually bothered by it, but he liked that Callie was standing up for him, even if it was true. He did have an overpriced club.

"I tend to have a blunt way of speaking." She gave him a cool look.

"Nice to meet you, Brooke. I don't have a problem with candor."

She didn't linger over the handshake. Then he looked at Callie. "It's good to see you, neighbor. Glad you decided to come have some fun instead of holing up in your loft."

She nodded. "I was curious about the place. It's much bigger and noisier than I thought it would be."

He got close to her so he could hear her over the clash of the music. He got a whiff of her heavenly scent and was glad it was noisy in here. Gave him an excuse to get closer. "Yes, it's loud and big. I have a special VIP room that's a little quieter. Would you enjoy that more?"

"It's really nice," Harper said above the music.

"All right. Let's go."

He gently set his hand against the small of her back and ushered her toward the room. They went up the metal stairs and through the door. He leaned over and said quietly to his door employee, a huge guy named Bubba. "Clear it out, discreetly."

He gave him a nod.

The ladies followed him inside and the throbbing beat of the music cut off as the door closed. Inside it was low, but lively.

They settled into a booth and he subtlety cut Brooke off from getting between him and Callie. He liked the brunette's sass. Callie smiled at him sweetly while Brooke looked worried.

"What have you been up to, Harper?"

"Oh, you know, this and that."

"Schmoozing at fundraisers, making the party scene, shopping, and jetting around the world?" He smirked.

She laughed out loud and it was contagious. He was sure that no one made fun of Manhattan's Darling.

He gave her a sly grin and she shook her head. "How about you, Owen? This and that, too. Like redheads, blondes, and brunettes?"

Okay, this was why no one teased Harper. She had her claws out and was just as determined as Brooke to spoil his fun.

"Meow," he said softly, and unperturbed, Harper took a sip of her drink. Brooke high-fived her with her eyes and Callie gave her a censoring look.

"Oh my God. This is beautiful. What is it?" Poe said, looking around, quite impressed with his club. This goth girl might look like a biker chick in that black, studded leather, but she was possibly sweeter than Callie and as adorable.

"Techno classical. Vivaldi, one of my favorites," he said as a waiter came to the table. Owen said, "Scotch." He didn't have to tell the man how he liked it. Everyone knew it was Glenlivet, neat. "Truce," he said, "Ray bring the ladies each a snifter of the Tres Belle."

Harper froze and said, "You bastard." Her friends looked puzzled. "I wouldn't sell my dearest friend out for Tres Belle, but it's up to Callie."

"What is Tres Belle?"

"Cognac," Harper said with a melting tone. It's more than a hundred years old, very expensive, very smooth and it's my favorite."

"Truce," Callie said. He grinned.

Poe grabbed Callie's arm and said, "Come dance to this with me. As she went by, she grabbed Brooke's arm, too. He was alone with Harper.

She leaned forward. "What are you doing, Owen?"

"Nothing. Just showing my neighbor and her friends a good time. Maybe they'll spread the word."

"Something's getting spread and it's not vowels and consonants," she said sugary sweet.

His eyes narrowed. "I don't have designs on her, Harper."

She smiled, but it had nothing to do with mirth. "Then you're not in touch with yourself."

He looked away and tried to get himself under control, the anger her words generated ignited by the truth he harbored. She leaned forward a little more. "If you hurt her, I swear I'll cut out your beating heart and when the crows show up, I'll feed it to them, then lick the blood from my fingers."

"There's red on my white truce flag." Aching for the first time in a long time, he said casually, keeping that anger banked, "You taking over for the Queen of the Damned?"

"I will in this case. I mean it."

The cognac arrived, a deep ruby red in the cut crystal glass. Harper never even looked down. He took a sip of his scotch to unclench his jaw. His eyes going unerringly to Callie, and something in him turned over. He'd never felt this way before, and it was killing him. He'd pursued whatever woman he'd wished, never discriminating between them, but she was different, and he wasn't sure he could expose himself to her.

He didn't do vulnerable and guarded his past like it was full of gold which couldn't be farther from the truth. He knew what exposing himself would entail and the darkness of his past pressed on his soul as black as the raven from Poe's namesake's poem. He wasn't sure he hadn't lost his soul a long time ago before Great Aunt Matilda had a chance to save him.

Callie couldn't keep her eyes off Owen. Oh, Lord, he looked good tonight. He was having an argument with Harper. It was clear he was on the defensive, but Harper did that to people. But, suddenly she could see something in his eyes that was…devastating. She couldn't stand by while this was happening. She left Brooke and Poe, went back to the table, slipping in beside him. There was a tense silence and Harper pushed away from the table, joining Poe and Brooke.

He looked at her, regret deep in his eyes. "Maybe these vouchers weren't such a good idea. Enjoy your evening," he said, softly then rose and walked away. She switched her gaze to Harper. Their eyes met, but that woman was unrelenting when she was being overprotective. She picked up the cognac and left the booth, following Owen out a side door and down the hall. A door closed, but Callie wasn't going to let a closed door stand in her way.

When she reached it, it opened into a panoramic of the city. There was food set up on one table and she was starving. Owen was leaning against the handrail that kept patrons away from the glass.

He turned as the door closed around him, his face thunderous. But it smoothed out the moment he saw her. She went to the table and set the glass down. Picking up a piece of French bread, she scooped up a generous amount of caviar and took a bite. She might not be a glamourous party girl, but she loved caviar. Popping the rest of it into her mouth, she polished off the bite.

He turned back around, his broad shoulders stiff. "Harper can be difficult," Callie said. Picking up a hors d'oeuvre, she savored the delicious taste of bacon, cream cheese, and ham. Reclaiming the glass, she walked across the room, stopping beside him. Absorbing the beauty of New York City lit up. She turned toward him and said, "She's just being my mother hen, even though I can take care of myself."

He turned to face her and took a step toward her. "Can you?" He looked dangerous all of a sudden in the dim light, his mouth unsmiling, a dark intensity in his eyes. "She thinks I'm the wolf and you're Little Red."

"I'm not."

"Maybe so, but I am a wolf. So do yourself a favor and steer clear, babe."

"You're warning me? I thought we were friends. We have the puppies to deal with."

He groaned and rubbed his hand over his face, then slouched against the rail. "I actually forgot about that." He eyed the glass in her hand, then straightened. "You going to hold that or try it. It's an experience," he whispered.

She turned toward the window, and he moved behind her, the smell of her making him forget about what he'd pledged only hours ago.

He stepped into her. Owen thought of self-discipline as something he'd cultivated during the worse times of his life. Courage, honor, sanity.

He felt none of those. He felt only her hair beneath his jaw, springy and fragrant. It fascinated him because it was so soft. He couldn't move. If he moved he would plunge his hands into it, bury his face in it. He would pull her against him, into him, bring him to his knees, engulfed in the hot, dark tide.

She tilted her head back and he said, "For the love of God, don't."

He lifted his hands, not quite touching her. Her body seemed velvety, pressing along secret curves and paths. His was as hard as hers was pliant, his blood pumping faster.

He tried to back up, but she turned, framed in the neon of the lights that pulsed outside, illuminating the darkness. She pressed against the handrail, and stared up at him as if she was caught in a magician's spell, tilting her head, exposing her throat, her hair falling down behind her shoulders, lit by the window so that red and gold played amid the caramel—a sight that exploded inside him, sent force and weakness to his fingertips.

While he stood there paralyzed, she said, "Don't what?"

She was an innocent babe, and he didn't want her to be. He wanted her to be like him, scarred and tangled, so he could pull her down to the floor and have her, her delectable mouth on his, her laughter, her warm, satiny body smothering him. He wanted it, but he couldn't take that because he would hurt her. He knew he would.

He'd move on like he always did, and he would leave her broken.

But she looked up at him with those dusky green eyes, her fine delicate features that comprising a face that haunted his dreams.

He stood there wanting to touch her like a compulsion akin to addiction. Her voluptuous scent, the sounds. His own throat tightened with a suppressed moan. He wanted only to hold her, cradle her against him and he wanted to overpower her. There was a terrible violence inside him. All he knew, all he had experienced and mastered in his life couldn't light the darkness in him. Will and shame kept it in check, but will failed him.

Shame ruled him.

His past seemed like fantasy and mist, and he had never been alive until this instant.

This must be a soundproof room because she couldn't hear anything but her own heart. Was she a fool for coming here and trying to comfort him? Maybe, but she couldn't seem to stand the look on his face. He moved forward forcing her to move back until she was cornered between New York City and a sexy wall of muscle and heat. Before she could move the glass to her lips, he took it from her and said, "Let me help." He took a sip and before she could figure out how she was going to get a taste when he was drinking her liquor, he pressed his mouth to hers.

She opened on a soft gasp, her body melting at the feel of his firm, gorgeous lips, burning with the heady taste of flowers on fire. As soon as she opened up, he plunged deep, warmth exploding on her tongue. The rich taste of…cherries, plums, the aroma of it soared through her nose like seduction. The aftertaste a sweet burn, like peaches cooked under an open flame. Then, through that aromatic liquid, the rich, aching taste of Owen, deliciously male, flavored with the ripe fruit of his passion. She groaned, and he broke away from her. Swore viciously and threw the glass against the far wall, the liquid running red against the white.

Without another word, he backed up, something on his face and in his eyes that both inflamed her, made her want to hold him, made her need the feel of his bare skin against hers. But he said, his breathing harsh and uneven, "I'm sorry. That was wrong, a mistake," he murmured as if Owen McKay, the baddest bad boy in New York City had lost his charm, his sanity. He whirled and strode out of the room, the door slamming behind him.

"Owen," Callie said, weak and breathless. He couldn't possibly hear her. He was gone. After he'd planted one on her hot enough to melt her into liquid, he'd left. Her insides dropping away to nothing, Callie felt instantly bereft. She had brought this on by fantasizing about her neighbor, even after she'd sworn off men who would love her and leave her.

What kind of fool was she?

"Callie?" she heard Harper's distant voice. She stared at the closed door and immediately pushed herself off the handrail and tried to compose herself. She didn't want those women to worry about her. Owen had made it perfectly clear that he considered her a mistake. Of course. She wasn't his type.

Then why had he kissed me like that?

She had no answer just a pain blossoming under her breastbone that was going to spread and then leave her desolate if she let it. This was counterproductive. She had to interact with Owen, Jill was carrying Jack's offspring and he owed it to her parents and to her to discuss this impossible situation.

On shaky legs, she walked toward the door getting stronger as she got closer. She took a deep breath and let it out. Opening the door, she followed the music back to the VIP Room. Harper gave her an exasperated look. "Where did you go? I was worried."

"Just to the amazing viewing room with a panoramic of New York City."

"With Owen?" she hissed. "That's his seduction room. "What happened?"

Callie smiled. "Nothing. Geez, Mommy, give it a break." Her insides were tied in knots, her heart breaking at the look on Owen's face and even though she knew she had to hit this head on, she couldn't shake the feeling that he was harboring some serious pain. She clasped Harper's arm. "I'm fine and you need to take it down a notch. He's not a mean or terrible person, sweetheart."

Harper sighed and nodded. "I know. It's just that I couldn't bear to see you hurt, Callie."

"I'm not going to get hurt. I'm going to be smart."

Harper smiled and wrapped her arm around her and hugged her hard. "You are the sweetheart," Harper said. "I'm a bitch in an expensive dress."

"No, you're not." Callie said, hugging her back. "You're a cosmopolitan, assertive woman who has had to deal with assholes most of her life."

"Okay, so you're a perceptive sweetheart."

They left his club without another glimpse of him. Harper's limo was at the curb and they piled inside. Poe couldn't stop talking about how much fun it had been. Callie was still reeling from the taste of Owen's mouth, his unique flavor that made her crave more.

She closed her eyes and let out a breath. Harper hadn't stopped giving her those looks. She knew something was up, but Callie wasn't about to tell her. She wasn't going to say anything at this point.

After they dropped her off, she took Jack out for his walk before they settled down to sleep. Back inside, she looked at Owen's door and with a sigh went inside. He probably wasn't home yet. It wasn't even midnight. It would have to wait until tomorrow.

Callie was up and at Sit Happens at her usual time, but she stewed the whole morning. At noon, she told her manager she would be gone for a couple of hours.

She grabbed a cab home and with determination, went up to her floor. Knocking on Owen's door, she took a fortifying breath as it opened.

He stood there looking like he'd been drinking heavily. He winced when she said, "You look like hell."

"Not so loud," he murmured.

"Look. We'll forget about last night. It was a lapse in judgment. Don't beat yourself up because this Little Red is just fine."

He squinted at her. "Geezus, Callie." He ran his hand through his hair.

"I want you to come by and meet my mom and dad. She will want to look at Jill and talk about this situation. We can go this weekend if you're free." He just stood there rubbing his temple. "Oh, for the love of God." She brushed past him and walked through his loft to the bathroom. Opening the medicine cabinet, she grabbed a bottle of ibuprofen. Shaking out two tablets, she grabbed the glass on the sink and filled it to full.

She shoved both into his hands as he stood in the doorframe watching her with pained amusement.

"You'd think a nightclub owner would have the common sense to head this off at the pass with pain medication and water *before* he went to bed. You're dehydrated, you idiot. It's called a h-a-n-g-o-v-e-r—hangover. Be ready on Saturday morning. I'll drive."

"Anyone ever tell you you're pushy?"

"Yeah, the dogs complain all the time. Want to know what I tell them?"

"I'm afraid to ask."

"Use the suggestion box." She started out the door and turned around. "And, believe me, it is only a suggestion. The owner has the right of refusal."

She slammed the door on her way out, figuring he deserved the shot to his head and went back to work.

Later on that afternoon, Callie paced while Brooke groomed a small fidgety poodle who was muzzled. Callie couldn't understand how something that small could be so dangerous.

"I'm taking him out to Harrison tomorrow."

"Is that why you're so agitated? I have to admit he wasn't anything like I thought he would be," she said. I thought he would be arrogant and smug." She blew out a breath. "But he was charming and...I don't know...vulnerable. Now I'm confused. Thanks for that." She went to clip the dog and she growled, snapping inside the muzzle. "But Harper took him down a notch. That was pure Harper."

Callie stopped pacing, wondering exactly if Owen deserved the rap he was getting. He had been the one to pull away last night, to smash that glass as if he wanted to cut himself. "Yeah, she was rude and so were you."

Brooke sputtered for a moment, then sighed. "Okay, I was slightly rude, but I was trying to have your back."

"I know, Disapproving Mary, Mary quite contrary. But we have this problem between us that has to be resolved."

"Once it is, shouldn't you steer clear of him?" Brooke said with warmth in her eyes.

"Great Danes gestate for sixty-three days on average. That's three months, Brooke," Callie whined.

She bit her lip. "Can you resist him that long?"

"I seriously don't know. I'll do my best, Commander Mary."

"How about lunch," Brooke said. "My treat." This was a blatant olive branch and she really couldn't blame her friends for being so worried about this situation with Owen. Callie had been devastated in college several times until she'd wised up. So why was Owen different from all those guys with chips on their shoulders, the ones that were almost irresistible? Could his bad boy charm be an act?

"Something light. My mom is making peach cobbler."

Brooke groaned. "I wish I had my afternoon free. I'd go with you as a buffer."

"Who you kidding? You want my mom's cobbler."

"Guilty. I'm very sad."

"How about I bring some back for you?"

She brightened. "I knew there was a really good reason we were friends."

The next day Callie sat at the curb in her lime green Jeep Sahara and waited for Owen. She'd already strapped Jack into his doggy seatbelt, folded the seat down so that the two Danes would have plenty of room, and removed the roof panels above the driver's and passenger's side. She was a bit apprehensive remembering that fierce, sultry kiss he'd given her. She didn't want it to be awkward. She hopefully diffused that already.

The day was full of sunshine and warm for October in New York. Orange, red, and yellow leaves rustled in the breeze.

Owen emerged with Jill on a leash. Jack got agitated the moment he saw her. "Keep your pants on, Jack. She'll be here in a second." Her tone was soft.

Owen opened the back door and the dogs greeted each other happily. "Settle down," Callie ordered, and Jack folded down on the seat. Owen strapped his excited dog into her restraint, and when she immediately obeyed his firm command for her to sit he turned and beamed at Callie like a proud papa.

When the passenger side door opened, Callie got the full impact of Owen. He was dressed in beautifully made but more conservative clothes than usual—in deference to her parents, probably. He also smelled delicious. The idea that he might want to impress her parents made her melt inside. He smiled as he settled into the seat.

His dark hair was just touching the collar of a navy-blue crewneck sweater over a white polo, the sleeves pushed up his muscled forearms. His pants were slim-fit gray, a light summer-weight wool, and his shoes a high-shine black oxford with a contemporary blue sole. He looked sharp and successful.

"This is a crazy color for a Jeep, but it suits you."

"What? Its sportiness?"

"Yes, you have that fresh, girl-next-door, tomboy thing going." His voice dropped an octave and his eyes traveled over her from the baseball cap on her head to the tight denim encasing her thighs, to the brown cowboy boots on her feet.

Her pulse kicked up a notch. Coming from any other man, the tomboy remark might have offended her, but from Owen it sounded like he found her sexy just the way she was. "I hope that was a compliment."

Owen's smile came slowly. "It was meant as one. I can't say I've met anyone like you before."

That gave her a big boost. "I'm one of a kind," she quipped to lessen the escalating tension.

"That's the problem," he said softly as he sat back in his seat. She pondered that for a moment, decided it was a powder keg that was best left unlit, and put the Sahara in drive.

CHAPTER SIX

HE TRIED TO FOCUS on the city as they passed through, but no matter how hard he tried, Callie stole his attention. Unfortunately, both dogs had fallen asleep on the back seat, so he couldn't be distracted with making sure they behaved. As they approached the I-95 North exit, he said, "Tell me about Lassiter Run." His voice came out sounding a little desperate, demanding. He shifted in his seat and inwardly groaned. That kiss last night had been...his brain fogged over just thinking about it. He still wanted more, this whole keeping his distance thing not working at all.

He cursed at the fact he wouldn't be in this situation if he'd gotten rid of Jill. At first that was his thought. He had no room in his life for a dog. But she was the last thing, besides him, his great aunt had loved. He could live with the inconvenience, but not the guilt. He'd kept the dog. And because of that, he was now in this situation with Callie. If he could have kept his distance, maybe…maybe he could have resisted her. Yeah, and if he had a lick of sense and the brains God gave a goat, he wouldn't be in this situation at all.

She glanced at him before she merged onto I-87 and smiled. "Next to the city, it's the best place on earth."

All of his childhood had been spent in the city and some of those years were with his dysfunctional mother. When she left one day and didn't return, he was a lost boy, wandering mean streets as he tried to survive. But his great aunt had never stopped looking for him and rescued him. Even with all his travels as an adult, he hadn't seen much of the rest of New York State.

"Lassiter Run sits on about thirty acres. We have twelve kennels and nine dog yards, along with puppy runs we use to segregate the older dogs from the little ones. We exclusively breed Danes of all colors. But I, of course, have a soft spot for Harlequins."

She wasn't his type. In spite of reminding himself over and over, the attraction between them pulled so hard he swore he'd be leaving a trail scored by his heels on the lawns of Lassiter Run.

"Does your family show the dogs?"

She glanced and him, then back to the road. "My mother does. She's even been to Westminster with Jack's sire."

"Did she win?"

"A couple of times. Did your great aunt ever show Jill?"

The scent of her filled up all the space in the front seat and it was as if he was surrounded by flowers, each whiff only making matters worse. He cracked open the window, needing the respite. "No, she didn't get the chance. She had pancreatic cancer, and she grew too ill to leave the house."

"Oh, I'm so sorry."

He nodded and looked away. He still couldn't seem to stop the well of emotion each time his great aunt was mentioned. The deep grief he felt for her passing had been compartmentalized, like everything else in his life. It was as if his hip, cool persona took everything he had in him to maintain. Letting emotion show, any emotion, would set off a feeding frenzy among his fellow sharks. That wouldn't bode well when he was presently working the currents of the deep ocean and its shadowy predators. His backers would pull out with any whiff of weakness. They expected certain things from him, like his reputation, having beautiful women on his arms, fueling the publicity train. Right now it felt as if that locomotive was a runaway.

He felt her touch on his arm. When he looked at her, he saw that genuine concern deep in her dark green eyes. "I'm sorry. I didn't mean to upset you. It's so hard to lose a loved one." She squeezed his arm, and his heart turned over. "When we lost my grandpa, the grief would sneak up on me when I least expected it for more than a year. It was as if the memories were all bundled up inside with nowhere to go. With no outlet, it just feels as if those memories sit on your heart and shred it."

His breath caught and moisture pricked at his eyes. No one. Not one person of his acquaintance had offered him the tiniest bit of comfort when his great aunt had passed, and yet this authentic, goodhearted woman had already seen through his façade and offered him not only comfort, but sympathy, in a wise and touching way.

It threw him off his game. Usually, with a woman he wanted, it was all heat and seduction. There was never any substance to those relationships, and he had preferred it that way. Preferred the women who were seduced by his face, body, status, or wealth. It made everything so much easier, so much less…weighty. He had no doubt he could seduce Callie into bed and that kiss had proved it. Even now, his body tightened at the thought of how she would feel against him, how her mouth would fuse to his.

So he was trapped for the time being. However, what it amounted to was yet another compelling reason to steer clear of her. Thanks to this dilemma with Jill and her pregnancy from a prized potential stud, he couldn't ignore the protocol. The owners had a right to check out his dog. They had a right to be concerned about her offspring.

He also recognized that Jill had to have some training. He wouldn't be in this predicament if she had been spoiled less and disciplined more. Again, Callie could help him. So, for sixty days at most he would have to interact with her. Jill's puppies would be born by then, and Jill would be sufficiently trained. He could go back to just being her neighbor.

"But if it doesn't help to talk about it, I'll try not to mention your great aunt."

"If you have questions, it's all right to ask them, Callie. It's true that her passing has been hard, but I wouldn't stifle your curiosity. She was a wonderful lady and deserves to be remembered with respect and love. I was lucky to have had her, to have known her and to have been loved by her." He was quite shocked at the words that came out of his mouth. Callie squeezed his arm again and then was distracted by maneuvering the Jeep through traffic. He had to take a moment to regroup. Never had he revealed so much to anyone.

This was the danger with Callie. She was so easy to talk to and for a man who wanted to keep his armor directly in front of his heart, it was risky. She seemed to breach it as easily as breathing.

She pulled into a long drive that led up to a large house with kennels. Two posts held a green and blue sign that said Lassiter Run in bold letters.

The big Victorian was a real showpiece, with a riot of fall flowers planted along the beautifully maintained walk. Pumpkins were scattered here and there, along with multi-colored corn husks which decorated the front porch posts. Little pumpkin lights were strung along the eaves. Baskets of spider mums hung from the porch's rafters, and rockers invited guests to sit awhile and enjoy the company of friends. It was very homey and inviting.

A tall, sandy-haired woman came out onto the porch, flanked by a fawn adolescent Great Dane and a full-grown brindle.

She waved to Callie with a wide grin on her face, and it made his heart ache just a little.

Callie jumped out of the vehicle and both dogs launched themselves off the porch and sprinted to her, greeting her joyously with barks that woke both Jack and Jill. He noticed how well the Lassiter Run dogs behaved. Neither one jumped up. She petted them, and then told them to stay as she raced up the steps and gave her mother a big hug.

Owen felt as if he was intruding on her private time, but she motioned him out of the Jeep. His palms sweaty, he wiped them on his pants before getting out. Jill whined when he shut the door, but he ignored her for now.

He approached the stairs, and Callie's mother eyed his face, then his clothes. She narrowed her eyes at Callie, but the younger woman just shook her head.

"Mom, this is Owen McKay. He's my neighbor in the city."

Callie's mom reached out her hand and said somewhat cautiously, "Hello, Owen. Welcome to Lassiter Run."

"Thanks, Mrs. Lassiter."

She waved her hand with a warm light in her eyes. "Oh, please, call me Kate."

He nodded.

"To what do I owe the pleasure of your company?"

"Someone told me you were making ham, scalloped potatoes, and a peach cobbler," Callie said slyly.

"Oh, Ian has such a big mouth." Callie's mom said affectionately.

"Yeah, it's too bad he can't be here, but he's got a show to get ready for."

"I understand," she said looking from Owen to Callie.

Callie glanced at him and took a deep breath. "Mom, we're here because, well…Owen has a beautiful Mantle Great Dane bitch."

"Oh, how wonderful. Did you bring her with you?"

"Yes," he said looking over his shoulder at Callie's Jeep. "She's in the car."

"Mom," Callie said, and the note of trepidation in her daughter's voice made her focus on Callie.

"What's wrong?"

"Well, we happened to walk our dogs at the same time and they got a little excited to see each other. They escaped together for about an hour."

"I see."

"Owen had just inherited her from a family member, and he wasn't aware she was in heat."

"Oh, dear. She's pregnant by Jack. Is that what you're trying to tell me?"

"Exactly."

"I'm so sorry, Mrs…Kate. If I could fix this, I would." He really was sorry about this situation and not just because he wanted to avoid Callie. He was genuinely concerned about Jill, the integrity of their breeding program here and handling a pregnant dog.

"Well, it seems that the fixing should have occurred before she got pregnant," she said with a laugh.

Owen's anxiety lessened by degrees at the open and amused look on Kate's face. He chuckled and so did Callie.

"Owen didn't mean for it to happen. I'm sorry that Jack got his dog pregnant. I should have been more vigilant."

"It was an accident. What kind of agreement have you come up with?"

"Owen has offered us the pick of the litter."

"That sounds fair," Kate said, putting her arm around her daughter's shoulders. Then she turned to him. "Owen, not to sound elitist, but what is Jill's pedigree? I'd also be very interested in her medical records. Danes can be prone to hip dysplasia, and other types of diseases and abnormalities that make any dog that has them a poor candidate for breeding. We're very careful in our breeding program to maintain the highest quality, both for our Danes and for the breed as a whole."

"I can appreciate that. I brought her papers and medical records for you to look at. She does come from championship stock." Owen pulled the papers from his back pocket.

Kate took them and started reading. She nodded her head as she read. "Oh, nice! Champion Martin Lacy's Coal Black Miner for her sire and Champion Hollywood's Marilyn Monroe for her dam. Excellent dogs. I know Hollywood's owner personally, but am only acquainted with Martin and Lacy Ball. I see she's registered as Martin Lacy's Jill St. John Diamonds are Forever. I know that Lacy is a big fan of James Bond movies. That all seems to be in order. She also has a clean bill of health. Well, get her out of the car and let's take a look at her."

He nodded and walked back to let the dogs out. Jill jumped down and was instantly greeted by the rambunctious puppy and the brindle who looked almost exactly like her.

"Callie, take Lila and Summer back into the house." Callie reached down and awkwardly scooped up the seventy pound "puppy" and gave Summer a hand signal. The dog fell into step with her. It only took her moments to return.

Jack made a beeline for Kate and gave her plenty of kisses when she knelt down. Giving him gentle pats, she said, "It's nice to see you, too, Jack. Looks like you have been getting yourself into some mischief. Let's take a look at your sweetheart."

Kate approached the dog, but didn't make eye contact, and Jill stood easily, smelling the wind. When Kate touched her, she didn't react, and Callie's mother nodded in approval. She ran her hands on either side of her muzzle, then the head and the neck down to her back. She nodded again and her expression eased some. "Could I see her move, please?"

Owen clipped on her leash and ran with her to the edge of the house and back. Kate watched with an intent expression on her face, and then she smiled.

"Well, I've got this to say. If you ever want to show that dog, she would be a champion. She's regal and graceful. She has a beautiful, full, square jaw with a deep muzzle, and a long, well-arched neck. Her croup slopes perfectly. Her temperament is also good, but if she's a bit unruly, Callie could probably help you with the training. She's top notch."

"We haven't agreed on a time," Callie said.

"I appreciate your graciousness regarding this situation with our dogs," Owen added. "I can assure you that I'll take very good care of her while she's pregnant." He meant every word.

"I'm sure you will, and thank you for the offer of the puppy. I'm not really sure what the protocol is regarding accidental pregnancy in purebred dogs, but this will suffice. I think we might get a Harlequin out of the litter."

"Why don't you show Owen the kennels?" Kate continued. "You can leave Jill here with me and take Jack to see his daddy. He's in number six. Dinner will be ready in about an hour."

"Okay, Mom. Jack," Callie called. Jack looked at her, then at Jill, as if undecided. Her mother gave Callie a wink and a soft smile.

"Ah, he's torn between his two ladyloves. Hold onto his collar, and I'll take Jill into the house."

Callie grasped Jack's collar, but he didn't even try to bolt. He whined softly when the door closed behind Jill, but obediently followed Callie as she turned to head toward several fenced-in areas that had numerous dogs in each.

One was full of puppies of all different sizes and colors frolicking on their long, gangly legs. Callie stopped and they came running to the gate. She petted a few and moved on. When they had walked for about ten minutes, they came upon a pen that held a regal Harlequin. His ears pricked and he came alert as he saw Callie and Jack. With a soft woof, he bounded toward the gate. Callie laughed as he pranced around impatiently while she unlatched the gate and let Jack in. Father and son exchanged greetings. When that was done, it was Callie's turn, and she obediently obliged the reigning champion of Lassiter Run with long strokes along his head and back.

"I can see why this is a championship Dane. He's magnificent."

"Yes, he is. And he's a good boy. Aren't you, Samson?"

She rubbed the dog's face, and he clearly reveled in the attention. Her hands were strong and sure, the slender fingers buried in the dog's soft fur. "Samson?"

She smiled at Owen's confusion and gave him an indulgent sideways glance, her green eyes animated. And once again, he had to remind himself that she wasn't his type.

"That's his call name," she explained. "Registered names are a formality. Sometimes dogs will be called a variation of their registered name like my friend Harper's standard poodle, Blue, and others, like Samson, are called by a totally different name. He's named after my grandfather, who built this kennel and passed it on to my father."

She bent down and picked up a ball. Both dogs stood at attention, and she hurled it across the run. Four hundred pounds of muscle dashed after it in long-legged strides.

Callie wasn't hard on the eyes. That was for sure. And he admired a woman who didn't mind getting her hands dirty. It appeared she wore little or no makeup, and had pulled her long brown hair into a ponytail beneath the baseball cap she wore as easily as some women wore diamonds.

Long hair. He liked that. It had looked so sexy loose and free around her shoulders. He was a guy, after all. But it was clear she wasn't all that caught up in the more conventional rituals of being female. Actually, Owen unapologetically enjoyed that extra emphasis on femininity in the women he chose to spend time with. Tomboys had their appeal, but he typically preferred a woman who embraced her femaleness.

The dogs came bounding back, Jack proudly displaying the ball for his mistress. Callie threw it several more times. Finally, she said, wiping her hands on her jeans, "Let's leave Jack here, and I'll show you the kennels. They're probably empty right now, because the weather is good, so they're all in the runs."

The kennels were immaculate, with deep green trimmed lilac hedges that would shade the kennels to keep them cool. Baskets of pink impatiens hung from the extended roofs that protected the walkways and kennels from inclement weather. About halfway down the first row they came upon a man hosing out one of the kennels.

"Dad."

He gave her a brief, one-armed hug. "Hello, sweetheart. Who do we have here?" Now he understood Callie's search for commitment. Who wouldn't want this. He clenched his jaw and told himself sternly. *You!*

Before he'd met Callie, he would have thought this didn't exist. Was some kind of fairytale.

"This is Owen McKay."

Her father reached out his hand, his eyes speculative. "Hello, Owen, welcome."

"Thank you, sir." Owen shook his hand, her dad sizing him up.

His eyes cut to her with a perceptive gleam. "Call me Daniel."

"We're here because Jack got Owen's dog pregnant."

His brows rose and he chuckled. "Oh, ho, what did your mother say about that?" His eyes sparkled.

"She checked her over, and she's fine with it. Jill has a great pedigree."

"That wouldn't have mattered. We would still have embraced those little rascals. My wife is very careful with the breeding, and if she is satisfied, then so am I."

"It was a total accident," Callie said slipping her arms around his waist and hugging him tight. He rubbed his hand up her back and kissed the top of her head. She really had some upbringing with two well-adjusted, hard-working, loving parents.

"These things happen, honey." He looked at Owen. "Are you staying for dinner?"

"Yes."

"Wonderful. Giving Owen the tour?"

"She has been, and you have a very nice facility."

He beamed and she glanced at him thanks in her eyes. He couldn't have said anything nicer to her dad. Maintaining his family's legacy was obviously very important to him. "Thank you. We try. I'll let you get back to it."

As they walked off, her father called out. "Callie, before you go, could you grab a screwdriver out of the tool chest in the shed?"

"Sure. I'll be right back."

Callie led them to a small structure situated under a sycamore tree. She pushed open the door and ducked inside. He followed. The shed looked as though it had been built by hand. "Did your father build this?"

Callie pulled up the lid of the toolbox. "No, my mother did."

"She did?"

"Don't sound so surprised," she said as she looked up at him. "She redesigned this whole kennel, too."

The light slanted in through a small window and fell on her face. The dancing sparkle in her eyes captured him as effortlessly as a beautiful view. Just like the night he'd kissed her in FLASH.

His breath hitched a bit when she looked down again and rummaged around in the toolbox. Her brown hair came alive in the sun. Golden highlights mixed with rich chestnut glowed with color.

She scowled and dug deeper into the box. He stepped closer, partly to be nearer to her, and partly to see if he could distract himself by looking for the elusive screwdriver.

"Don't be a sexist," she said, giving him a censuring look and nudging him with her shoulder. Body contact is not what he needed right now. No, but it was what he wanted.

"I try not to be. It's a guy thing. We automatically think that anything this well-built must have been done by a man."

"So, you're really more egotistical," she said with a grin.

He tried to remember that she wasn't his type. Remember that they were neighbors and that it was stupid to get involved with someone who lived that close. She was a sweet, commitment-type girl, the sort who set off his alarms. But either the volume was turned down, or he'd gotten too used to hearing them, because for some reason he couldn't seem to heed those alarms at the moment. Wholesome and down-to-earth described her perfectly, and seeing where she grew up only solidified his assessment of her character. He'd had no idea how seductive wholesome could be. Then, of course, his guy mind started wondering how sweet she would taste. How that taut little body would feel, would respond to his touch.

He leaned across her to check a specific part of the toolbox, caught her clean, fresh scent. She turned her face, and it was so close to his. He glanced down to her mouth and felt control simply evaporate.

CHAPTER SEVEN

"IT MUST HAVE BEEN amazing growing up here," he said softly, his face much too close to hers. His eyes were heavy-lidded, the blue peeking out from ridiculously long lashes. This close, his eyes were still really blue, cobalt maybe, a color that seemed to intensify as he looked at her, his pupils dilating. His skin was incredibly smooth, despite the hint of five o'clock shadow, with such a gorgeous golden tone that she imagined it would always be naturally warm to the touch. And yet the angles of his jaw, the hard line of his nose, his chin, the arch of his brow, all combined to make him more rugged than pretty. Made her want to touch.

Where was that damn screwdriver? "It was. What about you? What amazing place did you grow up in?" Her voice came out soft and wispy. She felt her resolve slipping. She tried to imagine Brooke's concerned and supportive face, but her vision was full of Owen and his seductive, bad boy mojo, a face that could wreck any woman's resolve, and a hard, muscled body that begged her hands to smooth over its hard planes.

He looked away, presumably to focus on the contents of the toolbox. His body tensed and his eyes shuttered. "I grew up on the streets until my great aunt found me and took me in. It was a hard-knock, learn or die type of existence, and didn't include any expansive lawns, drowsing puppies, or pretty hanging baskets full of delicate flowers. It was gritty and dirty and terrifying."

For a moment, the harshness of his statement shocked her. But when she recovered, her heart tilted. He meant it, too. This was the pain he was harboring and he figured she would be turned off by his background because hers had been so wonderful. His blunt confession gave her a glimmer of why he was a man who pursued many women but never settled on one. She didn't want that insight, because it made it just that much more difficult to resist him.

She wasn't sure he was telling her this to shock her, create distance, or gain sympathy. Little did he know that she was a sap for all things orphaned or in need. Not that he was either of those things, but still, she couldn't imagine a life without the strength and wisdom of her parents. She had a haven to return to, and support every day, even when she wasn't present. It was a comfortable safeness that permeated her life. Maybe that was why she sought out these kinds of men, the ones on the edge, to experience a bit of that thrill, some of that danger.

"I don't know why I said all that. Maybe I feel too comfortable around you. You're so open and caring."

She moved to the workbench and rummaged around there. "You say that like it's a bad thing. It's not."

"I've experienced the caring from my great aunt, but I've never trusted it." His tone was uneven and filled with some bitterness. He moved over next to her, searching as well.

She looked over at him, feeling even more sympathy. "Never?"

He shook his head, his eyes caressing her face as he stood close to her in the swath of sunlight from the window.

"I'm sorry for you, then."

"Don't be. I might be cynical when it comes to relationships, but I've done just fine alone. What about you?"

She moved some wires and hoses, but still no screwdriver. "What about me?"

"Relationships. You believe in happily-ever-after and saying I do—"

She turned to him again, "I never said that."

He looked down. "But you believe it."

She looked at his mouth, tried to focus on the conversation. His lips looked firm and soft at the same time. "My parents have had a long, happy marriage, so I've had wonderful role models."

"No broken hearts?" he asked, bringing his gaze back to hers.

She shook her head. "I've had my share, but I was young and susceptible."

Owen blew out a breath, tunneled his fingers back through his hair, looking like she'd just kicked him in the groin. "To men like me?"

"If I'm being honest, yes."

"By all means, be honest. It makes it easier."

"Easier for what."

"To know the ground rules."

Callie's jaw tightened against the first wave of disappointment. "Oh, Owen. I *know* your ground rules."

"Do you?" he asked in a low, graveled voice.

She turned her back to him to look at the far end of the work surface and to hide her disappointment. "Yes. No commitment, a fun time while it lasts. Everything free of messy entanglements."

"You *do* know the ground rules. And yet you still get hurt."

She lifted a shoulder. "Can't help how I feel. Controlling emotions is pretty much an illusion. Managing them is closer to the truth."

"But ultimately you want what your parents have."

She went past him and sighed. She would just have to tell her dad she couldn't find it. Besides, this discussion with Owen, although important, was making her feel terrible. He touched her shoulder, and she whirled, exasperation clear in her voice. "Yes, I want what my parents have. Who wouldn't? The bond, the support and commitment they give to each other is priceless. They are each other's best friends. And I guess I wouldn't settle for less than that, either."

He smirked and she wanted to slap him. "So you just trifle with men like me while waiting for Mr. Right?"

She bit out, "I don't trifle with anyone, Owen."

His face grew serious that smirk fading. "I can see that you don't. That was the wrong word choice. I apologize."

She looked away knowing that most of his life had been fueled by looking out for himself. Even with his great aunt's influence, Owen was running from commitment not because he didn't want it, but because he was afraid it wouldn't last. His wounds went deep and she'd be a fool to try to change a lifetime of his convictions, especially when he had so much evidence to back it up. "Apology accepted. I assume you can say the same thing."

"I don't trifle with women, Callie. I make sure they are all aware of my limits going in. There are no surprises."

She choked down the knot in her throat. "Right. We wouldn't want that. Well, I'm not that naïve young girl anymore."

He took another step closer, and her breath suddenly felt trapped inside her chest. So much for being brazen.

His voice was low and silky. "Still, you're not my type."

She didn't back down, and his comment didn't offend her. She might not be the most experienced person in the world when it came to relationships, but she knew his focused, intent gaze wasn't of the innocent variety. "Who are you trying to convince? You or me?"

He stepped closer still, crowding her against the workbench, the search for the screwdriver as lost as she was in his eyes.

"Fuck if I know."

His eyes were so dark, so deep, she swore she could fall right into them and never climb out.

"I think you're the girl next door, sweetheart, and I should leave you alone."

"And what? You're the big bad boy I should avoid at all costs? I think that *is* a good idea. I've sworn off bad boys," she whispered as his head descended and her breath backed up in her throat.

He lifted his hand, barely brushing the underside of her chin with his fingertips, and tipped her head back. "Have you?" he asked, his voice nothing more than a rough whisper.

His mouth settled on hers like kindling to fire, and ignited. He backed her up so she was pressed against the workbench, but she barely felt the wood digging into her spine. She was too busy feeling Owen McKay's mouth moving over hers with a sensual pressure that made her blood sing. Then she heard a deep groan and realized, distantly, that it was her own.

Her arms slipped around his neck, her forearms against hard shoulders, her fingers sliding along the back of his neck and burrowing into all those thick, dark waves. He pressed his hips into hers, growling just a little, as she ran her thumbs over his rough cheeks.

His heavy chest pressed tight against her tingling breasts as she welcomed the heat of his desire in the cradle of her hips, eliciting another growl deep in his throat.

His muscles flexed as if he was going to push away, his head lifting. When their lips broke apart, he looked dangerous and angry. Then his mouth covered hers again, taking her lips in a flurry of deepening, sensual kisses that made her head spin.

He trailed his fingertips from the pulse point in her throat all the way down to the tops of her breasts. Sharp awareness flared in her belly and spread through her bloodstream, triggering a slick, erotic warmth.

His mouth followed the path his fingers had taken, until they brushed the tops of her breasts.

"Callie?"

He reeled away from her as her gaze went to the door of the shed. Frantically, she snatched up her baseball cap and jammed it on her head. And that is when she saw the screwdriver sitting innocently on top of the workbench beneath some rope. She snatched it up, and called out just as the door opened.

"Found it."

"Excellent," her father said. "Now you can get back to what you were doing then wash up for dinner."

Callie almost snorted. She knew her father hadn't meant fusing their lips back together, and, as she looked over at Owen, she could see the same thought emblazoned across his face. But it was fraught with too much…just too much.

Oblivious to Owen's attempt to get himself under control, Callie's father strode out of the shed and let the door slam. Owen braced his hands against the workbench, the muscles in his arms bunching beneath the sweater. With a quick pull he yanked the sweater off, his face flushed, his breathing slowing.

"You heard the man," she said, trying to ignore the way Owen tracked her as she stepped out of the shed.

Callie had just dropped the keys on her hall table when she heard a noise from her kitchen. "Who's there?" she called out. She glanced at Jack, but he didn't growl.

The rest of the day with Owen had been fun, but strained. Her insights into his psyche made everything more difficult instead of better. He hadn't said anything during the drive home about the kiss, so Callie let it go. Instead, they made plans for him to bring Jill by on Monday to get her started on her training.

She simply couldn't get involved with Owen. She was already much too interested in him personally, which was even more dangerous than sexually. She realized she couldn't seem to disconnect the two, and that could only lead her to heartache.

"It's your brother, and he's hungry. Don't you ever keep any food in this place?" Ian groused in a good-natured way.

She smiled as she walked into the kitchen. "I haven't had a chance to go shopping. I forget how grumpy you get when you don't eat, Ian."

The fridge door was open and her brother had his six-foot-four frame bent over, peering inside. "Yeah, and I'm sure your tummy is full of Mom's good food. Did you bring any cobbler home?" He absently stroked Jack as he searched.

The container she was carrying did have two servings of cobbler in it. Her brother's eyes lit up, and he straightened and grabbed for it.

She pulled it away from his grasp. "But it's for Brooke."

"Oh, damn." His face fell. "Then I'm out of luck. I swear you're more loyal to those women then you are to your own brother."

She bit her lip. She shouldn't be a glutton. She had two servings after dinner. "Oh, all right, you can have the one I was saving for tomorrow on one condition."

He leaned back against the fridge and narrowed his eyes. "I don't like throwing games."

"One wouldn't hurt. Throw those guys a bone."

"All right, one game."

"If I had known you would be dropping by, I would have brought more home."

He eyed the container. She went to the cupboard, pulled down a plate and dished up half. Popping the lid back on, she said, "Did your meeting end early?"

"A bit." He eyed the container, but Callie gave him the stink eye as she put it in the fridge and firmly closed the door. She handed him the plate and a fork. He dug in, humming in pleasure.

"How about we order pizza?"

His eyes lit up. "That sounds good."

Callie picked up the phone and put in the order. "So did you just show up for food?"

He cleaned his plate. She was surprised he didn't lick it. Of course, it often crossed her mind. "Not exactly."

She went into the living room and he followed. "That sounds ominous."

From the doorway, she saw him rinse the dish and put both the fork and plate into the dishwasher. He turned to look at her. "There have been a few thefts in the building. The tenants think it's someone who lives here. It's not good for business, so keep your eyes open and be careful."

She walked to her stereo system and picked a CD, sliding it into the player. Soft tones of jazz filled the room. "Yes, I heard some women talking the other day about a stolen pillow. I thought it was an isolated event."

She sat down on the couch folding her legs under her. "No, there's been more, a quilt, a hand-woven rug, and a dinosaur comforter off a kid's bed."

Ian settled into one of her comfortable chairs across from her as Jack lay between her and the coffee table and set his head on his paws. He made a soft rumble in his chest and she reached down and fondled his silky ears. "Sounds like someone is opening up a soft goods store."

"Well, I thought about hiring security. But it's a thief of opportunity. One woman braced her door open to bring in groceries, and the other woman's kid left his ajar when he went to a neighbor's to play."

She sank back into the cushions, removing the ballcap from her head and pulling out the binding, releasing her hair. "Do you think security is necessary? So far this person hasn't been violent."

Ian shrugged looking concerned. "Maybe not. I don't like my tenants to be uneasy."

She smiled at him. He was so awesome. "Listen to you. Mr. Landlord."

"Shut up," he said good-naturedly, then smiled. "I have a vested interest in this property, sure, but when I first bought it, I also wanted to create a place where people feel safe, secure, and comfortable."

"Your vision was a good one," she murmured, getting sleepy.

Ian stretched and reclined back, setting his feet on the ottoman. "I actually thought about making this whole floor one big loft. In fact, I had plans of knocking out that wall over there and combining these two lofts, but decided the income would be better than the space."

She sat up straight. "Well, Owen McKay loves his loft, so no breaking out any walls while he's living there."

He gave her a sly look, his hands resting on his chest. "I wouldn't dream of it. He's a good tenant."

She sighed and pushed her hands through her hair, ruffling it with her fingers. "I should tell you, since you'll find out sooner or later, but his dog is pregnant and Jack got her that way."

Ian's sleepy look was replaced with wry amusement. "What the hell? I thought Mom and Dad were waiting for Jack to mature."

Callie snorted. "I'd say he's matured."

Her brother chuckled and rose, kneeling down to cup Jack's face and run his thumbs over his features. "So this was planned?"

Jack made a soft sound and closed his eyes at the stroking attention. "No, it was an accident, and Owen feels so bad."

The sly smile was back. "Owen, is it? You know that guy is a major player?"

She frowned. "I know, and don't go all protective older brother on me. I have no intention of getting involved with him."

"Hmm. You looked pretty acquainted to him in the bar the other night." He eyed her. "The best laid plans…"

"Now it's time for you to shut up." She shoved his shoulder and he retaliated by getting her into a headlock. They tussled for a few minutes.

The doorbell rang and her brother reached for his wallet as he headed for the door, "Saved by the bell. Well, be careful is all I have to say in both situations."

After spending an uneventful Sunday, Callie was ready for work on Monday. At eleven on the dot, Owen and Jill entered her training facility. Callie was finishing up her puppy class, and as she said goodbye to her students, she kept an eye on Owen.

He looked good today, with the tail of his shirt tucked into dark jeans and the cuffs rolled and pushed up his forearms.

After the last student left, Owen came over to her. "Are you ready for us?"

She wasn't sure she was ready for Owen and the potency of his presence, but she was ready to teach his unruly dog some manners.

She nodded and walked over to a bench in the ring where she taught most of her classes. She settled down and patted the seat next to her. "Let's chat first about Jill."

"All right."

"So, I gather she was pretty much indulged from the time she was a puppy. She hasn't been taught the basics."

"That's right. I can't even get her to sit, but she did offer Poe her paw. So my aunt Tilly must have taught her that."

"I can guarantee she'll sit on command before you leave today."

"I have no doubt. This is, after all, Sit Happens."

She shook her head as she fought to ignore his charming banter. "Most humans don't realize that dogs are not people. Dogs are dogs and they're pretty simple. Their natural instinct is to want structure, rules, and boundaries. That's why there is a hierarchy in packs. They each know their place and where they stand and how to behave. When they step out of line, the pack leader makes corrections. That's where you come in. You're the pack leader. Right now, Jill doesn't respect you. She won't listen to you because you haven't taught her you're the boss."

"I get it. A dog responds to the owner's ability to understand him and give him what he instinctually needs as a dog."

"Correct. Once you start setting some boundaries, it'll get better. Let's start with teaching her how to sit.

"Here is a treat," Callie continued. "Hold it in your hand, but let her see it. Keep saying sit until she obeys, then give her the treat. This will probably take several tries."

She watched as Owen worked with Jill and was impressed by his patience. It was too bad she couldn't forget how his mouth felt on hers or how she reacted to him as a man. But she would be either an idiot or a fool to believe that a relationship with him could go anywhere.

It was time to find something lasting and real. Flings were something for a younger woman with less experience. She wanted mutual trust and commitment. By Owen's own admission, he could give her neither.

There was just that niggling doubt. Could it be because he'd had such a tough life when he was young? Could it be that he was afraid to take those steps because he'd been hurt and abandoned?

The thought gave her pause, and she did conjure up Brooke's words of wisdom to help her. But Brooke didn't know his circumstances. She knew her nurturing friend's face would soften after hearing Owen's story.

She watched as Jill almost got it, but Owen tried one more time, and then she did it and the look on his face was priceless. Callie cheered and clapped. Owen rose in one powerful push of those thighs and wrapped his arms around her. She hugged him back, caught up in the simple breakthrough.

Then the hug changed. She felt the tension in his body and the innocent moment of victory changed into something lethally charged. He felt so wonderful, as if he was the intricate, hard-to-find puzzle piece that just...fit. She didn't want to let him go, but she knew she must. He pressed his face against her, the warmth of his skin and breath seeping into her pores and igniting a raging fire. Trying to hang onto her control, she closed her eyes against a rush of passion so intense her whole body clenched.

They turned their heads at the same time, seeking what each of them craved. His lips brushed across hers. Warm, a little soft, but the right amount of firm. He slid his fingers along the back of her neck, beneath the heavy braid that swung there, sending a delicious little shiver all the way down her spine.

He dropped another whisper of a kiss across her lips, then another, inviting her to participate, clearly not sure how she felt. But she wished that he wouldn't be tentative, wished he would make the decision final and then she wouldn't have to berate herself later. He lifted his head just enough to look into her eyes, a silent question in his own.

She met intensity with intensity, but she knew that it would be a mistake to get involved, even though the man made her body literally hum.

"You said it was a mistake the first time. How about the second?"

"Insanity?" he offered.

He saw her refusal to continue and backed off. "We should have talked about this...thing between us."

"You mean the chemistry?"

"Is that what it is?" he asked with a smile.

"Isn't it? We click. That's all. I just need something...more."

He nodded. "I understand. But I have to say I have regrets."

"It's better than me ending up with a broken heart," she said softly. "I said I understood the ground rules. But I think I'll pass instead of play." She took a deep breath and had to ignore the disappointment on his face, the reluctance in his eyes. "So, now that that's settled, let's focus on Jill. The most important, best thing you can do for her is take control and keep it. She will test you. That is her natural instinct. Pack leaders lead, and that's what you need to do. If she exhibits any type of behavior that you frown on, teach her the behavior that you want instead. She really does want to follow you. Exert that control. You'll have a much happier dog, especially now that she's going to have puppies. She wants to make sure her environment is safe. Also, I want you to consider something."

"What is it?" he asked his voice subdued.

"I think Jill would benefit from agility training. She has a lot of energy, can jump like a dream, and has a lot of coordination for a Dane."

"Agility training?"

"Yes, it's an obstacle course. There are even competitions."

"No kidding." He paused. "Okay, I'll consider it. But would it be safe for her while she's pregnant?"

"I wouldn't have her hurdling, but she looked pretty comfortable jumping over your couch. I would suggest some basic stuff. I think she gets into trouble because she's active, intelligent, and bored a lot of the time. It couldn't hurt to start teaching her the very basics. All I'm doing is asking you to consider it."

"I will, seriously. So next week, the same time?"

Callie nodded. "I'll see you then," she said with feigned brightness. When he walked away, all she felt was longing, and most likely the same regret he was feeling.

She arrived at Cibo Molto Buono, a high-end Italian restaurant in Hell's Kitchen. Brooke was already seated, but Harper and Poe hadn't arrived yet. She waved to Brooke as the maître d nodded and escorted her to the table. When the waiter asked her for her drink order, she requested a glass of Merlot.

"You're drinking wine." Brooke's words came out more like an accusation.

Callie shrugged, trying to keep it light and casual. "So?"

Brooke's eyes went darker with worry. "Something's up. What's wrong?"

Callie forced a laugh, her insides twisting into knots. "Nothing."

"You only drink wine when you're upset." She grabbed Callie's wrist and turned her toward Brooke.

"I'm not upset," she lied.

"Why is Callie upset?" Harper asked as she sat down and flagged the waiter.

"I'm not upset," Callie insisted.

Poe came to the table and noticed the tense atmosphere, then eyed Callie's glass of wine. Callie wished she'd just cancelled the dinner.

"What's up?" Poe asked, her shoulders tensing.

"Callie ordered wine," Harper and Brooke said in unison. It would have been comical if she wasn't busy fighting against the need to tell her friends about what had happened with Owen and how she was faltering.

"Oh, no. What's wrong?"

"Spill it," Harper said.

"Oh for the love of Pete," Callie said. "I kissed Owen McKay."

"Where?"

"On the mouth."

"No where were you when you kissed him?"

"The first time?"

All the women groaned. "I kissed him at the club when we were together in the panoramic room, and I took him to my parents so they could check out Jack's pregnant girlfriend."

"Oh, cozy family home. That was bound to happen," Poe said. "Well, you got it out of your system. Now you can move on. There's a cute doctor I could set you up with." Poe gave her a bright smile.

"Not exactly."

"But he's real cute."

"No, not the doctor part, Poe, the getting-it-out-of-my-system part."

"What is that supposed to mean?" Brooke asked.

"She kissed him again," Harper said.

"I kissed him again," Callie confirmed.

Brooke sighed. "When?"

"His lesson. He was teaching Jill to sit, and he got so excited he hugged me, and I hugged him, and then all of a sudden we weren't just hugging. We were *kissing*. But I was firm afterward. I told him that a relationship wasn't going to work."

"There's only one thing to do now," Harper said, her voice dire, and her expression grim.

"What?" the other three women asked in unison.

"You're going to have to sleep with him."

CHAPTER EIGHT

YOU'RE GOING *to have to sleep with him.*

Harper's proclamation was still reverberating in her head as she returned from another dismal date. The cute doctor only wanted to talk about all the interesting surgeries he'd preformed in great and vivid detail. The jerk asked nothing about her job and nothing about her.

Letting herself into the loft, she responded to Jack's greeting and then threw herself down on the sofa. With his usual uncanny ability to sense when she was down, he gently placed his head in her lap and gazed at her soulfully.

You're going to have to sleep with him.

She clutched her head and said miserably. "Stop it voice."

Harper had explained that to get Owen out of her system once and for all, she'd have to sleep with him. Get the sex over and then she could move on. That's what this was all about...the anticipation. Once that was satisfied, she could forget about him. It was good in theory.

Except it wasn't the sex she anticipated when she saw him. Sure, the heat and the physical stuff was on her mind, who wouldn't think about getting into bed with Owen, the man was a gorgeous, hard-muscled babe. But it was about seeing him, being with him, enjoying his company that was just as anticipatory as the possibility of consummating their physical desire.

Jack made a soft distressed sound in the back of his throat. "It's okay, Jack. Things will get better." She pressed her face against his.

Except that she hadn't been able to find her Judith Leiber cream clutch. The last time she had used it was on her previous snooze date. She'd set it on the foyer table. But when she went looking for it to use on this date, it wasn't there. She decided she must have put it back in her closet. She would have to search.

A knock on the door startled her. She released Jack and looked at her watch. It was close to eleven. She called out as she got off the sofa. "Who is it?"

"It's me, Owen."

Her pulse jumped, but she tried to ignore it, and the way her heartbeat skittered.

When she opened the door, he looked worried.

"What's wrong?"

"Jill. I think she's sick."

Callie had opened the door too wide, and before she could stop him, Jack slipped out and made a beeline for Owen's loft and the open door.

"Jack!"

Callie took off after him when he didn't heed her call. Inside Jill was dancing around him.

"Oh. She looks fine now. But she's been off her food, and she was really lethargic today. I thought she was sick."

"Well it looks like the big hussy just needed a shot of Jack."

Owen chuckled. "Looks that way. I'm sorry to get you out of your apartment so late. You look nice."

She blushed and smoothed her hands down the little black dress she wore. She liked the mix of flirty and chic. She would have thought as a grown woman she'd be over it, but, no. She actually blushed.

"I was...ah...on a date."

"Really?" he asked. He frowned, held her gaze for a few more seconds, then looked away, his fist clenching. "Did you have a good time?"

"Poe set me up with one of the doctors at the vet hospital."

He nodded. "A doctor. That's great."

His tone of voice conveyed how not great he thought it was. She wasn't going to confirm for him that it hadn't been great at all. That all she'd done the whole evening was compare the poor man to Owen. It was best to let Owen think she was involved, because, dammit, he was just as enticing now as he had ever been.

"I should get Jack and let you get some sleep."

"I'm somewhat of a night owl. I don't open up the club until about six."

"Oh. I see. I don't open up until ten, so that gives me some leeway in the morning. It's nice. Well, I should go anyway."

"Do you have to? I mean, Jack and Jill need some bonding time. Maybe we could let them be together for a bit and we could play cribbage."

"I've never played it."

"I can teach you."

"I have some crackers and cheese at my place. Should I get them?"

"Sure."

Callie rushed next door to get the food and change her clothes, putting on sweats and a T-shirt. In the meantime, between episodes of kicking herself for being an idiot, she assured herself that the dogs did need some time together. Jack was looking way too droopy. It was all about the dogs. But a little unheeded voice kept saying, "Yeah, riiiiight." It was only a coincidence that the voice sounded exactly like Brooke's.

Owen greeted her with a plate and knife.

"Sorry to disappoint you, but I don't have a cheese server. I guess I'm not that cosmopolitan."

"Well, I wouldn't say that. I've coveted this plate set from the Pottery Barn. Especially the skull one with the creepy saying, Midnight Dreaming."

"That's my favorite one, too. Does that say I have a little pirate in me?"

"I'd say there's plenty of pirate in you, Owen."

"Well, then get to chopping, wench, the crew be hungry."

She tried not to be swayed by his devilish charms and excellent pirate inflection, really she did. "Aye, aye, Captain," she said with a mocking salute.

"Show some respect, woman, or it'll be the plank for ye."

She laughed and stepped away from him a bit—no need testing her swayability by putting herself in actual contact range—and sliced up the cheese and laid out the crackers. She kept her back to him, all the better to avoid being caught up in those deep blue eyes of his. "I should warn you that I'm a pretty fast learner."

Owen came to stand beside her, picking up the platter of cheese. She put the knife down. She knew her limits. Bracing herself, she looked at him. Up close like this, almost as close as they'd been in the shed when he'd kissed her, it was impossible not to get caught up in his intensity. He didn't even have to try. How he worked that lazy smile with those laser beam eyes of his, she had no idea. But anybody fooled by his easygoing demeanor was just that, a fool. "Is that a challenge?"

"It is." She took a deep breath as he tilted his head and narrowed his eyes. Who was she kidding? At least learning a new game might keep her from fantasizing about what she really wanted to be doing.

"Okay, then you're on. Have a seat. Would you like wine?"

She settled down at his beautiful, smooth, blocky teak table. Mixing Owen and alcohol would be a very dumb move. She watched him open the fridge door and bend down to look inside. Her gaze followed the line of his body, but got stuck right at the seat of his jeans, drawn over his…ah…yeah. Water was a much better idea—poured over her head. Make that very cold water.

He grabbed two wine glasses and set them and the bottle on the table. At that point she decided it wasn't wise to put up too much of a fuss about the wine. After searching briefly in a drawer under the TV, he came back with a square piece of wood with three columns of colored peg holes and a deck of cards.

He set the cards down on the table and opened a metal slide at the bottom of the board. Three pegs dropped into his palm. He kept out the red and blue pegs and placed the green back inside the board, sliding the metal closed.

Next, he set the pegs in the peg holes at the beginning of the board and shuffled the deck. He placed it face down and said, "Pick a card."

Callie pulled the ten of diamonds and Owen got the seven of clubs.

"That means I'm the dealer, and you go first. This game is based on numbers. We'll alternate laying down the cards. The face cards are worth ten points and the other cards count for their numerical value. Seven for any seven card, and so on. The goal is to get the most number of points. If your cards add up to fifteen points when you lay down your card, you'll earn two points on the peg board.

He dealt out six cards. "Okay, now you have to decide which of your cards you'll put into what's called the crib. The object is to give me a lousy crib, but don't mess up your hand to do it. Don't give me pairs or five-cards, stuff that could easily add up to fifteen."

She looked at her hand and chose the cards she would give him.

They started to play, and she felt she was getting the hang of it. He won the first hand.

"So, how did you get FLASH started?"

"I started small, and I paid celebrities to host the opening of the club. Small potatoes at first, then I expanded and was able to start hiring A-list people. My great aunt helped me with some of the startup capital. It did so well that I was able to pay her back. Now celebrities come to my club without being paid."

"That's the sign of success."

"How about you? How did Sit Happens happen?"

Callie laughed as she scored two points with a fifteen and pegged her points. "Of course I've been around dogs all my life, and part of having dogs is making sure they behave, especially with so many dogs in our kennel. I fell into it and learned about how to speak dog from a young age. My parents helped me with the initial capital, too, along with my generous and successful brother. He's ten years older than I am, and came to the city fifteen years ago, just out of college. Needing affordable studio space, he and a bunch of friends formed a cooperative. They bought this building for almost nothing, and turned it into these terrific lofts, keeping the integrity of the architecture. When he made it big in the art scene, he moved to Soho. He's also my landlord."

"I bet he gives you a better rate than he gives me."

"I'm afraid so. Nepotism is a good thing. My brother was here the other day. Did you know that there have been thefts in the building?"

He shook his head.

"Well, be careful about security."

He nodded. The hand played out and her crib had no points. "You are good at this," she said.

"My great aunt taught me."

"It's always nice to have those kinds of legacies from your family. For me it's the dogs."

His face became somber. "I can only say I wish that were the case. We only started playing cribbage when she got the cancer. She was pretty much stuck at home through much of it, and then the hospital. I learned it to pass the time with her. There were moments I'm thankful for, and, unlike the visits before she was sick, meaningful. I wish I had visited her more often. I was always so damn busy."

She covered his hand as he picked up the cards and he looked at her with deep sorrow in his eyes.

"I can't even imagine how hard it was for you. But you did have a meaningful relationship with your aunt Tilly. I can see that. I can see that you feel terribly guilty about it, too, Owen. But there's no doubt in my mind that she loved you regardless. It's just what a nurturing person like your aunt would do."

For a moment he just stared at her, his dark eyes unreadable. "I've never met anyone like you, Callie. Most of the women I've been with wouldn't for a minute be content to talk and play cards while our dogs snuggle. I have to confess that I would never have said anything about Aunt Tilly to any of them."

She blushed again, the compliment one of the best she'd ever received from a man. It was better than the one when he'd said she looked nice. This was about her character, and it meant more.

Owen certainly wasn't making it easy for her to remember to keep her distance. She hadn't expected to have anything in common with him besides the dogs, and she still felt they were diametric opposites, probably in more ways than not. She hadn't gotten all that far away from her roots, whereas, while he might have had a rough beginning, he'd certainly gone a long way toward polishing off any rough edges from his childhood.

"Thank you. I consider us friends." She looked over at Jack sleeping curled up with Jill. Her dog was in love, head over heels in love. She could not go there with Jill's owner. And if she didn't want to start down that slippery slope, she'd better get herself out of here.

"I should go." She rose, and he did too. Coming around the table, he took her hand.

"I'm sorry. I hope I didn't make you feel uncomfortable."

"No. It's not that, Owen." She tried to keep a cool head even with the warmth of his hand clasping hers. "It's just that we have to agree to be friends instead of…"

Owen held her gaze for what felt like an eternity, and she wondered what he was thinking behind those inscrutable eyes. "Lovers." His voice came out soft and husky.

She closed her eyes briefly. "Exactly. So you see the dilemma. Nothing has really changed." It seemed that the most innocent conversation between them was going to have mixed overtones, and she wasn't sure how to stop that. And to be perfectly honest, she didn't really want to. It felt good. She had no business engaging in it, but that didn't make her want to stop.

"No. I guess not."

She went over to Jack and said, "Come on, boy." She walked towards the door and opened it.

"I don't think he's going to cooperate."

She looked over her shoulder to see that Jack hadn't done anything except lift his head.

She slapped her thigh and pointed next to her right leg. Normally, he would already be sitting there looking obediently up at her. She got exasperated, because not only was it humiliating in front of Owen, but she *was* a freaking dog trainer. She would have said that Jack was the most well-behaved dog in New York City. Now she couldn't even get him to come to her.

She walked over and grasped his collar, then strained and stressed, but couldn't budge him an inch. He not only wouldn't get up, but he pulled back. "Jack!" she said in her sternest voice and he flinched, but refused to make eye contact. He made a pathetic noise deep in his chest.

She bit her lip. It wasn't as if she was immune to his needs. But he'd had his time with his girlfriend and now they needed to leave. She pulled harder and finally he rose, but planted his feet and pulled back again. Owen watched her with laughter lurking in his eyes, but she failed to see any amusement in this situation.

When she straddled her dog, he laughed out loud, covering his mouth. She tried to walk Jack out of the apartment, but when she got about halfway across the room Jack collapsed, and Callie fell and rolled onto her back.

Owen was now laughing freely as he reached down and helped her up.

"He's really putting up a protest. How about we watch a movie and then try to get him out? He's obviously not ready to go."

"But I am. I'm ready to go, and he's being terribly stubborn. Ever since he met your dog, I've lost control of him."

"Come on," he chuckled. "Let's watch *One Hundred and One Dalmatians*. There's a bunch of really bad dogs. It'll make you laugh."

"You have *One Hundred and One Dalmatians?*" She arched a brow.

He shrugged, an amused glint in his eye that only made him that more appealing. "Well, yeah. I like Disney movies. So sue me."

She held up her hands. "No, I think that's pretty cute."

His lips curved a little and, too late, she remembered that part about his charm being more lethal when he was amused. "Just a bit of advice. Guys don't like to be called cute."

"Because, well, *One Hundred and One Dalmatians* is so…ahhhh…manly."

He grabbed her by the neck and pulled her close. "Shut up. You're hurting my feelings."

Callie laughed harder. "That's because you're so cute and precious."

They tussled for a moment until she accidently got him in the ribs and discovered he was ticklish. "Ah, the secret is out. Your Achilles heel."

"No, stop it," he warned. They collapsed onto the couch until he effectively restrained her hands. But it was too late, she was on top of him, her hair had come out of its ponytail, and the feel of his hard body beneath hers was totally distracting.

Harper's words came back to her then, and she almost leaned forward. *You're going to have to sleep with him.* It was an agonizing decision. She was torn between the promise of immediate, profound pleasure and the inevitable pain it would cost her. Now that she had gotten to know him, it would be even more difficult to let go. If they were physical, would it really get him out of her system?

He said nothing, just looked up at her with that hopeful expression on his face. She swallowed, grabbing hold of her control. She had promised herself she wasn't going to do this. Promised herself that she wasn't going to get involved with bad boys any more. She pushed off his chest and sat back on the couch. She saw him do the same. Without a word, he went and put in the disk and pressed the remote.

"I'm curious about something," she said, keeping her eyes on the TV screen.

"What?" he asked as the opening credits began.

"You said your great aunt thought that you were lonely. With so many people in your life, the club, the women, why would she think that? It baffles me."

A look of hollowness crossed his face and he turned to look at her. "You can be lonely in a crowd when no one really knows you or cares who you really are."

She met his eyes, then dropped her head forward, her hair covering her face. Finally, she nodded. "I see."

She started to pull her hair back and he touched her wrist. "Don't."

She let it fall. It was the only thing she would give him at this moment.

CHAPTER NINE

OWEN FELT the pressure against his chest. Even in sleep he knew it was good. He snuggled closer to the intoxicating, warm scent. Soft hair brushed against his nose and his eyes popped open. He found Callie's head nestled in the crook of his arm, his cheek resting on the top of her head, her sweet-smelling hair just below his nose.

The gray light of dawn filtered through his floor-to-ceiling windows. The busy city's racket lessened at night, so the volume of the traffic noise below made him think it was about six.

He'd had so much fun with her last night. It was a mixture of camaraderie and sexual need all rolled up into one achingly tempting package. She was truly a one-of-a-kind woman. Somewhere between his confession about his childhood and the easygoing nature of Callie, he'd lost something—the barrier that kept his emotions in check. He wasn't sure he could replace it now that Callie had gotten a foothold.

He frowned, remembering that she had said she'd been on a date with a doctor. He wondered if she planned to see the guy again. He was stunned at the intensity of the anger and loss he felt just thinking about another man wooing Callie. Owen wasn't usually a jealous man. It had been live and let live, but this time he felt differently. He felt differently about Callie.

He had to cringe when he thought about his past, with the parade of beautiful women in and out of his life. The club had given him the prestige he'd sought, given him the image he needed to fuel his reckless abandon, and provided plenty of women more than willing to fulfill his superficial and physical needs.

But somewhere between his great aunt's death and meeting Callie, something had shifted in him. Where he once reveled in the *Scoop's* "Woman of the Week" column about him, he now wished that they would move on to gossip about someone else.

Callie was a real, giving person. That's why last night he'd been hypersensitive to the sexual chemistry they shared. He didn't want her to think she was some kind of conquest, but he wanted the woman bad. His morning hard-on was inconvenient and only made matters that much worse. She shifted against him, and he could tell by her breathing that she was awake.

"Looks like we fell asleep. Would you like some breakfast?"

She stirred and her head fell back against his shoulder. "Even in sleep, I can't seem to keep away from you."

He smiled. His heart hurt, twisting with all the emotion trapped inside. He wanted to kiss her so badly, but knew that wasn't a good idea.

"Breakfast, like you'll run down to the bagel place kind of breakfast?" she asked.

He laughed softly. "You don't think I could cook a few lousy eggs and fry some bacon?"

"Wow. That sounds good. I'm usually a cold cereal kinda gal."

Callie moved away from him, and he just enjoyed watching her yawn and stretch, seeing the way her hair tumbled around her face, and the drowsy cast to her just-opened-eyes.

"I think I'll pass." She sat up, then looked over at Jack and groaned. "I don't think he'll want to budge. He looks so comfortable."

The two dogs were wrapped around each other in sleep, Jill's softly rounded belly triggering another wave of panic for Owen. No matter who told him that dogs have an easy time with birth, he worried about losing Jill. It was a tie to his great aunt and...dammit, he loved that dog. He didn't know when it happened, but it had. She had been a comfort on his bad days and a joy on his good ones. Now that he was agility training her as Callie suggested, it was even better. Callie had been right. Jill had an aptitude for it. She was picking up the basics pretty quickly.

"Why don't you leave him here? Bring me his leash, and I'll walk him when I walk Jill. You can let them have the day together. I'll be taking Jill to the dog park later, too."

"Are you sure?"

"Contrary to the evidence from yesterday, he is a very well-behaved dog. I don't think he'll give me any trouble. It's not like he can get her pregnant again." He thought about that for a second. "Can he?"

Callie laughed softly, the sound drifted through him like soft rain. "No. He can't." She looked over at Jack, smiled softly, and walked over to pat him. He raised his head slightly, thumped his tail, then went back to sleep. "The trainer in me just wants to take control and make him obey. It's a definite no-no, but this one small occasion shouldn't hurt. Okay. I'll drop his leash by. Thanks for looking after him today. I'll be home about four."

"No date tonight?" He hadn't meant for that to come out and he certainly hadn't meant to sound so…peevish.

She looked at him with a startled expression. "No, not tonight."

"If that doctor had any sense, he'd set up a second date."

Callie looked both amused and crestfallen. He knew he should say something about them dating, but he couldn't get the words past his barriers. It was better this way. She wanted commitment, and he just couldn't let his guard down.

"I'll leave you my key, too. Just in case you want to drop Jack off."

"All right."

First Owen took the dogs for a walk and laughed at the amount of attention they received. The Great Danes were so huge that just walking with two made him secretly feel like he was a giant among men.

Celeste came by late morning to discuss the inventory and restocking of the club.

"We are low on vodka, so I prepared a purchase order to restock," she said, leaning over him. She had found many occasions recently to brush against him or touch him. Nothing had ever been overt, but he knew when a woman was coming on to him.

For the first time in his life, he wasn't interested. When she stood in his path and put her arms around him, he was surprised.

"I got tired of waiting," she said softly before she tried to kiss him. There was no comparison. Where he completely lost himself in Callie, Celeste, for all her beauty, barely made a ripple.

He grasped her upper arms and set her away. "I made myself clear, Celeste. We're not going to do this anymore."

She picked up the papers and shrugged. "Can't blame a girl for trying."

"I'll get all this taken care of," she said with a disappointed look. "I'll see you tonight."

She left, and he knew that he would have to make sure she understood fully he wasn't interested. His emotions were a chaotic, raging mess. He would have to sort them out before he made any promises to Callie.

In the late afternoon, he heard some banging in Callie's loft. He looked at his watch and saw that it was only three-thirty, and she wasn't due home till four. He sat up straighter, wondering if the thief Callie had told him about could be in her apartment right this second. He left the dogs at his place and used Callie's key to let himself quietly into her loft. The banging was coming from her bedroom. He approached the closet door cautiously, until he heard Callie's voice swearing.

"Callie?"

There was a squeak and she came tumbling down on top of him, along with a rain of purses.

"What the hell?" he exclaimed, as he barely managed to catch her before they fell to the floor together.

"Why did you sneak up on me like that?" she demanded, pushing up on her arms and planting her hands flat against his chest so that she could look him in the face. Her face was flushed and her eyes were stormy. He'd never seen her like this before and wondered if she'd had a bad day at work.

The act of moving her torso away from him only pushed her hips into his. He gritted his teeth at the pressure on his groin. The woman was driving him completely insane, and he was about ready to beg her. "I thought you were the thief," he said, trying to keep his voice conciliatory.

"If that's the case, you should have called the police," she snapped. Her hips jerked around in her anger, and he couldn't stop his immediate biological reaction.

"I wanted to make sure," he said. "Why are you home early? You said four."

"Are you my keeper?" Her brow arched and she took on that dog trainer voice. He wasn't a canine, but he was smart enough to realize she meant business.

"Why are you so surly?"

Mild accusation glimmered in her gaze. "For your information, I was looking for my Judith Leiber clutch. It's vintage, and I think it might have been stolen by the thief."

"Is that why you're in the closet?"

"Yes, and I'm home early because it's your fault."

"My fault? Why?" He was immediately concerned about what he could have done to upset her. He preferred his smiling, funny, Callie to this angry, aggravated woman.

"I want you," she said breathlessly, leaning forward, grabbing the front of his shirt and tugging. His body, sensitized already by her gyrating hips, sprang to life, desire sizzling along every nerve ending.

His erection grew and she felt it. He saw the reaction on her face, in her eyes before she closed them. He shook with the promise of all that pent-up passion just waiting to be unleashed. "I couldn't think clearly today, because all I could freaking *think* about was you." Her hands kneaded his chest. "Waking up in your arms was an unbelievably tempting way to start my day. But I've sworn off men like you," she said, her voice strained. "I promised myself I wouldn't do it."

"And, now you want to break that promise," he murmured huskily.

"God, yes." When she opened her eyes, they were dark and keen with desire.

His patience snapped so completely he groaned with the need he'd trapped inside, the barrier he'd erected not only coming down, but he feared he was irrevocably changed. And her eyes widened in surprise when he flipped her onto her back amongst the debris from the closet.

He shook his head. "I think it's a given that most men don't really understand women, though I have made the effort. But you…"

She looked up at him, and the defenselessness in her eyes demolished the flimsy wall he had shored up. The barrier he'd had left over from his childhood, the one his great aunt Tilly had tried to gently coax down, fell with a thud as she touched his face, tracing her fingertips over his lips, his cheeks, his forehead.

"There's no need to figure me out, Owen, like some kind of equation. There's no math required. Just go with your gut."

"That's the problem," he said. "With you, everything is all jumbled up. Even the math parts."

Her face softened and her fingers paused in their exploration. "What are you worried about? I know what I'm getting myself into."

It wasn't the question that gave him pause. It was the immediate answer that came to mind. Did he know what he was getting himself into, or was it already too late? His head told him he didn't know her. His heart called him a liar.

"You are just so sweet. I just—"

"Don't want to get involved with your plain Jane neighbor? The owner of the dog who got your dog pregnant?"

"There is nothing plain Jane about you. *Nothing*. You cloud my judgment."

"It's a bit too late"—she nudged her hips against the solid length of him—"for second guessing."

He groaned at the move, and it took every scrap of will he had not to drive his hips into hers. He dropped his chin and swore under his breath. "I don't know what the hell to think anymore. You're driving me crazy."

She cupped his jaw and brought his face up with the soft cadence of her voice until he met her gaze. "Good. It's nice to have a kindred soul here in Crazyland."

He smiled a little at that. He couldn't help it. "My thinking needs to be a bit more focused if you want a way out of this."

"And here I thought getting us both naked was a good idea. It could be a great way to diminish all this sexual chemistry standing in the way of our…clear thinking."

"You think this"—he risked bumping the length of his erection between her thighs, catching his breath when she gasped, went a little more supple against him—"is all going to miraculously disappear, is that it?"

"Okay, so my thinking isn't all that clear right now," she managed with an intake of breath as he pushed against her again. "It was just a theory."

He pushed her head to one side with his chin, dropped his mouth to the spot below her ear. "Do you honestly think one time will clear things up?" He placed a hot, wet kiss on the side of her neck, then gently sank his teeth into her flesh, making her gasp and his body jerk. "Or do you think it will only make me want you naked and underneath me as often as possible?"

"I—I can't think." She dug her fingers into his shoulders and moved her head, allowing him better access to the responsive underside of her chin. "I just don't think ignoring it is going to make it go away." She sighed when he began to drop kisses along the underside of her jaw.

"No, probably not. But it complicates things, Callie. I'm not good with complications."

She was silent for a moment, then said. "I get that."

He paused and pressed his forehead against her cheek. His body was one big hard-on at the moment, but his heart... She had a way of tangling that up without even trying. "Do you?" he asked carefully.

"We have our own paths. We're adults. We're not kids anymore, with fantasy dreams and unrealistic expectations..." She paused, he waited. "I won't lie. I wanted you from the moment I saw you."

He lifted his head then, looked her directly in the eyes. "Callie—"

"I know what I'm asking for."

Trouble with a capital T, was all he could think and it affected both of them.

"Maybe even that is more than I can give."

"Maybe. But I think it'll be enough for me. For now."

They'd denied each other more than once. He'd like to believe he was tough enough to do the correct thing every single time, no matter how demanding. But he was aware that he wasn't perfect. And he also knew he wouldn't be perfect with her.

"I wanted you then, too," he told her, which made her eyes darken with need, her body soften even more in anticipation of him, and what was left of his resolve disintegrated.

He wanted to evoke that look in her eyes again and again. He wanted it when he was inside of her, when taking her up, when he pushed her over. He wanted to be the only one who saw that look, ever, and it was that vicious, outrageous surge of possessiveness that almost gave him back the distance he so desperately needed.

"I want you. You want me. It's simple," she said.

"Yeah," he said, his voice now rough with need, with impatience, and not a little uneasiness. "Yeah, completely simple."

She hadn't planned this. Not really. Okay, everything she said was totally true. She had been distracted, and as the day wore on, she got angry. But she hadn't been sure who she was angry *at*. But she guessed she'd made the decision already. Brooke and her friends probably would worry about her state of mind, but this wasn't about them. This was about connecting with a man she was attracted to, who made her heart beat faster. This was about both passion and friendship.

He'd said he wanted this, but he was still looking down at her. "Are we waiting for something?"

"I'm just...looking at you. Give me a minute."

She melted right then into a warm, gooey mess, like chocolate in a heated pan.

His thumb slipped over her lips, and she kissed the pad, pleasure followed by the punch of desire she saw in his eyes, which had already been almost swamped with it. It was heady, powerful stuff, knowing she moved him like this. She tried not to think about how ambivalent he'd been before. Logic and rational thought were not going to stop this from happening, anyway.

He rose, and she thought he was leaving, that he'd changed his mind. But the flutter of panic changed into more melting when he said, "I'm not going to make love to you on the closet floor."

She reached up and grasped his hand, and it was a short trip to the bed. She reached for the buttons on her shirt and he covered her hands and undid them himself. He removed the garment and unsnapped her bra, and she let it fall. She shimmied out of her khaki mini, pushing the panties off as she went. His eyes told her how beautiful he found her.

Naked in front of him, she reached for his belt and undid it. He closed his eyes as she undid the button and zipper of his pants and pushed them off his hips. His shirt came off last. His smooth, powerful body enticed her. She curved her hand around his face, reveling in the sheer pleasure of finally touching him as she'd wanted to do so many times. Slipping her hands into his soft hair, she pulled his head down to hers, kissing him hard, and he returned it with equal fervor. He pushed her back onto the bed, and then, in unspoken agreement, they paused in each other's arms. He tugged her hands from his hair and pinned them on either side of her, then slowly slid them upward, until her body bowed away from the mattress, pressing the tips of her achingly tight and sensitive nipples to the hard planes of his hot chest.

He crossed her wrists, then slid his hand down her arm, his gaze following, creating a second sizzling wake behind the stroke of his hand. He cupped her breast and kneaded it, his thumb grazing tantalizingly over her nipple. His gaze flickered up to hers as he gently pinched the tip. She gasped and arched into him, the exquisite sensations spearing through her, rendering her speechless as well as mindless.

"I've been dying to know how you taste," he said softly as he lowered his head. She could feel his warm breath brush against her oh-so-sensitive skin. She wanted to sink her fingers into his hair, urge him closer, and urge him to please put an end to the excruciating wait. But he continued his slow exploration until his warm, wet mouth captured her breast. She cried out as his tongue swirled around her taut nipple and the suction made her hips restless beneath his. He nudged her thighs apart with his knee, his mouth traveling to her other nipple as he let go of her hands to arch her back over his arm, pressing her more fully into him.

One hand slipped down over her rib cage, into the indentation of her waist as if he was memorizing every inch of her. Then it slipped over her hip to cup her butt. His other hand wrapped gently around her neck.

She groaned when his fingertips traced along her thigh and found her most sensitive flesh. Her thighs fell open, giving him better access as he intensified his sensual assault. Her hands clenched in his so-very-soft hair as his teeth nipped at her breast. She could hear her panting moans turn into soft gasps as she spiraled up and up…and finally over the peak.

She was shaking hard as his mouth covered hers, his kisses as intoxicating as his fingers had been. Nothing had ever felt this good.

"Callie," he murmured against her lips, "I don't want to stop, but—"

"Then don't." She brushed her fingers against the nape of his neck, and he groaned as he bucked against her, his shaft hot and pulsing.

"Protection," he gritted, his body tensing as she moved fully under him.

"Oh, God. I was so caught up…top drawer of the nightstand."

He did what was necessary. His body covered hers again. She could feel him literally vibrating with need. She wrapped her legs around him, opening herself for his thrust. His broad palms covered her hips as he glided into her. She arched, moaned, and when he began to move faster, she couldn't contain her pleasure. She'd had raw before, but with Owen it was basic, earthy…deeply satisfying.

She clung to him, both of them grunting as his thrusts surged deeper, faster. She wanted to slow things down, so she could remember every second, revel in every feeling, every sensation, but she couldn't even keep her eyes open to watch him. He was driving her up again, and she could only give herself over to it, to the powerful emotions and blistering sensations bulleting through her.

This is just sex. She reminded herself to make sure she didn't lose sight of the ground rules.

What she actually experienced was an irrevocable bond being forged, a union like no other. And it was Owen. Her fantasy finally come to life.

And then whatever thoughts she had scattered completely as he slowed, and she could feel his body coil, tense, pull back, all in preparation for what she knew was coming. It was enough to send her over yet again, the waning sun spilling against their bodies like stardust, as she gasped for air and gave back equally with every swollen thrust he made.

He was all but growling when he came, his hands holding tightly to her hips as he bucked against her. She gave herself over to him, reveled in his shuddering release, tightening around him to give them both every last explosion of pleasure.

He was shaking as he slid from her body and let her legs drop from around his waist. He rolled them both so that she was lying on top of him. The cool air of the loft felt good on her slick skin. Neither of them moved. The sun sank below the skyline as their heartbeats eased to a somewhat steadier rhythm. It was the only steady thing about her at the moment.

It felt good, she decided, being in his arms. Held so tightly, both cuddled and coddled. But she would have to admit that she had expected him to roll over, get up, say that was great, dress, and leave. Given his aversion to commitment, somehow she figured he would be cautious because his own emotions were in play. Maybe that was wishful thinking.

She had to prepare herself for it. She would have the sex she wanted with the bad boy, but this time she wouldn't let him break her heart. She'd be prepared.

She must have withdrawn then, in some way, because he tightened his hold slightly, then slid his hand up to lift her chin.

"Hi there."

She smiled at that. Men. Such a way with words. But it was the look in his eyes, a little amazed, but tempered with a lot of affection, that kept her from teasing him. She felt much the same way and wondered if he saw that in her eyes. "Hi yourself."

"That was…" He let the words trail off, but held her gaze, his own intensifying in ways that had her heart rate kicking up again.

"Agreed," she said softly. "It was."

He gathered her closer, settling her between his legs, so she was pressed against the full length of him, chest to chest, hip to hip. The soft places on her easing against all the hard planes of him. It felt remarkably fantastic, and far too perfect. She never wanted to leave, and she had to force herself to relax. She knew what was coming. He'd warned her this was what it was, nothing more. No matter how stunned and replete he looked.

"Hang on a second." He rose gently, and she slipped off his body. Reaching down into his jeans, he pulled out his cell phone.

"Ah, so you were ready to call the police."

He grinned. "Of course, but you have no idea how glad I am right now that it was you instead of a thief."

"Oh, I think I do."

His grin widened and, reaching behind her, he pulled her ponytail loose. Her hair fell around her face as he pushed a speed dial button.

His eyes never left hers and he said into the phone. "Hey, this is Owen. I won't be in tonight."

She heard the incredulous tone of the person on the other end of the phone.

"Nope, you handle it." He disconnected the call and cupped her face. His mouth found hers again and his hand delved into her hair, tugging her head back to get a better angle on her mouth.

She sank into him, her guard dropping a little bit, but not totally.

Later they fed the dogs, but left them in Owen's loft. Ordered dinner in and ate and laughed and made love again.

Her hair fell forward as he brought her mouth to his. "Owen, I want to feel your weight on me."

It caught his heart the way she said his name. It was deep and intimate. Callie was so true to herself, so open and sweet. She couldn't be anything else, and he wouldn't want it any other way. He shifted them both to their sides, paused there for a moment, kissed her, then moved the rest of the way, sinking deeply into her as she lifted up and wrapped her legs around his hips.

He closed his eyes. If he couldn't take this risk with Callie and try to give his heart, he'd be that kid on the street forever, never trusting, never giving, never growing.

He held her gaze in between long, slow kisses, moving inside of her, feeling her match his steady rhythm as easily as if they'd done this for centuries. He finally slid his arm beneath her, tilted her hips up that extra bit, so he could sink a tiny bit deeper, reach that spot he already knew was there, the one that made her gasp and tighten around him convulsively. The one he knew would take them both over the edge, as he looked into her eyes. "Callie…"

And those green windows to her soul grew shuttered then, at that one hoarsely uttered whisper. And it didn't scare him so much as hurt him. Because it felt like she was his, dammit, and it made him sick to think he might do something, say something to hurt her, and the look in her eyes confirmed it. Even though they both knew the reality of what they were doing to each other. Even as she pushed him over the edge. And where it would leave them.

CHAPTER TEN

"YOU *WHAT?*" Brooke's eyes narrowed, and she set down her martini on the polished marble surface of the bar at Colton's, an upscale Manhattan restaurant. They were out for Brooke's twenty-seventh birthday, and they had all ramped up their fashion game. The dark gray dress Brooke wore was typically conservative, but did have a flare of interest with the beads on the neckline, sleeves and hem. Brooke's dark hair was pulled into a severe bun.

Callie had promised herself she wouldn't feel defensive, but Brooke's look made her squirm. "I slept with him, so just get over it." Her own ensemble had been chosen with the help of Harper, who simply *knew* what Callie liked. So the coral organza thigh-length dress with a sporty racerback neckline and a skirt of oversized rosette appliqués fit her to a tee. Thinking about how

Owen liked her hair loose, Callie had actually taken the time to use a curling iron, though she'd had to borrow it from Poe.

"I told you it was going to happen," Harper said with a smug look. "Owen is charismatic and gorgeous." Harper was wearing a red, multi-tonal sequined dress woven with a lightning motif throughout with a red mesh jacket, the lapels red silk. Harper's tresses were a mass of golden curls. There wasn't a man who passed them who didn't gape.

"He's funny and sweet, too," Callie said, knowing she sounded defensive again.

"Oh, she's a goner," Poe said taking a long drink of her martini and looking very stylish in a one-shoulder snake print dress with a loose-fitting top nipped at the waist. The style of the dress revealed the raven tattoo just below her collarbone, fashioned out of the word *nevermore*. Poe's long, dark blue-streaked hair was pulled into a sleek, high ponytail.

Brooke groaned. "Are you sure about this?"

"I know what I'm getting into. I think he feels something for me." Callie hoped that her defensiveness didn't stem from any subtle sign she got from Owen.

"You have stars in your eyes, and I thought you were past all this, Callie," Brooke said, signaling the bartender for another round.

"It's not the same," she insisted. "I saw it in his eyes." She had seen it when he'd been making love to her. She was sure of it.

"Well, if you're really sure about this, I guess I can only support you with rocky road ice cream."

She touched Brooke's arm. She wanted her friends to be happy for her. Yesterday had been special. Waking up in his arms this morning had been seductive and cozy, none of that awkward morning after. They fooled around in the shower, and she'd been late for work. After walking the dogs, they had found it surprisingly easy to return Jack to her loft.

Brooke looked subdued and said, "I guess we're all susceptible to bad boys and irresistible men. Know that we're all here for you."

"I hope I didn't ruin your party."

"I don't want to see you struggle with the hurt and disappointment if this goes wrong." Callie looked across at Poe and Harper their expressions just as supportive.

"I think I'm going to head home," Brooke said. She gave Callie a hug and rose.

"I did ruin your birthday."

"No. I'm just tired and all this talk about sex and irresistible men makes me want to pop open the top of some rocky road." She gave Callie a smile. When she reached for her money, everyone waved their hands, shaking their head.

"Your money is no good here," Harper said. "Get a good night's sleep."

"You guys are the best. I'll see you soon." She left.

Callie couldn't help thinking that her sensitive friend, who might look as stern and starched as a nun cared about her.

"She's just upset," Poe said, switching seats and clasping Callie's hand. "She'll get over it. Right, Harper?"

Harper nodded. "She will. We're too close knit for her to stay upset too long. She's sensitive and caring."

"Nurturing," Poe said.

Callie couldn't help it. The guilt from ruining her birthday celebration was eating her up. Brooke wasn't like the rest of them. All of them had family, but she was alone, her parents barely remembered she was alive, let alone celebrated her birthday. That's why she was so close to Roscoe, her amazing bulldog. She'd had him for a long time.

The party broke up after that and Harper offered to drop her home, but Callie said she would rather walk for a bit, then she'd catch a cab. Both women tried to help, but this was something she had to work out for herself.

As wonderful as it had been with Owen, she didn't want to end up hurting either. It was one more layer of complication in their already complicated relationship. She walked through the city, nightlife hopping, revelers calling to each other in the street.

The stars were obscured by the bright lights when she looked up. The chill in the air making her breath fog. Finally, she lifted her hand for a cab and after a few zipped by, one stopped. She got inside.

"Where to, miss?"

Callie was about to give him her address, but instead, she said, "FLASH."

The cab pulled up in front of the club, which turned out to be fairly close to Colton's. How she was going to get in didn't worry her. She'd find a way.

The line snaked around the corner. The ornate wooden door was guarded by the same very big man who had been there the night they had used Poe's voucher. His shaved head gleamed in the streetlight glow, and the closer she got to him, the larger he loomed. No one was getting inside this club who didn't belong there. But then the doorman saw her and his eyes lit up.

"Miss Lassiter," he said removing the velvet rope and ushering her through. "Have a nice time." He readjusted the rope to the disappointment of the people at the head of the line. When she entered, the music was loud, and the place was full, with several celebrities, plenty of models who looked too young to drink, and tons of older, sharply dressed men to escort them.

She was just about to speak with the bartender when Celeste came out from a back room. She spied Callie, and then headed her way.

"Cassie…isn't it," she said, eyeing her dress like a cat ready to engage in a battle, her claws extended. "Don't you look…adorable. Like a frothy peach drink."

It was clear Celeste thought she was a little girl playing at being grown up.

"It's Callie, short for Calista. I'm looking for Owen."

"Are you?"

"Is he here?" She didn't have the patience for this woman's jealousy or her hostility.

Celeste stepped closer. "You know what kind of man he is and you're still after him? You must want a broken heart. That's all he knows how to do and I know that from experience, honey. If you were smart, you'd find another place to live."

Callie's chin came up. Already uncomfortable from her friends' reactions and her uncertainty about continuing her relationship with Owen, Celeste's words found a home easier than they would have a day earlier. Even though she knew Celeste's words were meant to hurt her, she couldn't seem to stop the prick of tears in her eyes.

"Just point me in the direction of his office, and I'll handle it from there."

"He's a very busy man," she snapped.

Callie brushed by her, determined to see Owen now. There was such a press of people in the place. She entered the door in the back and closed out the noise behind her. Most offices were usually in the back of the place. She'd just explore until she found him. She felt as if she could take her first breath since she walked in here. She moved down the halls past several doors until she came to an ornate double door. She knocked and walked in.

Owen was perched on the edge of his desk and there were three men, all dressed impeccably in suits, drinks in their hands. The conversation ceased and Callie steamed. Celeste knew he was in a meeting, and she hadn't said anything.

"I'm sorry," she murmured and backed out. "I shouldn't have come here without calling."

She backed away and turned to rush down the hall, Owen's hurried, "If you'll excuse me for a moment, gentlemen," barely registering.

She flew through the back door as Celeste gave her a smug look at the end of the bar as if she was waiting for just this moment.

If Callie wasn't so upset and embarrassed, she would have given the woman a piece of her mind. She rushed through the crowd, the tears at the backs of her eyes pressing hard. She was almost to the outside door when Owen's hand grasped her arm, halting her from exploding onto the street.

"Callie," he whispered as she turned, and he saw her face. "Babe, what happened?"

"I'm sorry about barging into your meeting. I didn't know you were busy."

"Don't worry about that. Why are you upset?" He tipped up her chin and his mouth tightened. "You're crying."

He wrapped his arm around her and started moving her back into the club. She tried to protest, but he soothed her and said, "Shh, it'll be okay."

Before she knew it, they were entering the panoramic room. The door shut behind them. He took her to a seating arrangement near the window and pulled her down with him on the sofa.

He cupped her jaw and raised her head, brushing at her tears, his face concerned, his eyes dark and intense. "Who hurt you?"

"I ruined Brooke's birthday party. They're all concerned about you." A whole avalanche of misgivings filled her. "Owen, this was probably a really bad idea." She pushed away from him and the soft look in his eyes was replaced by hurt. She didn't want that. She didn't want the people she cared to have in her life hurt, but her relationship with her friends was too important not to think about what she was doing with Owen.

And Owen, oh God. How could she catalog how she felt for him when this was just too new and untested? Except, she did feel something for him, something that was too profound to ignore. Torn and confused, fear starting to make her waver, falter. "Maybe we should take a step back," she whispered.

He stood and shook his head. "I don't want to take a step back. For the first time in my life, I want to pursue this beyond a casual relationship. Callie, I want that with you."

The air backed up in her lungs and she was even more confused and scared. He wanted to take their relationship to the next level? Beyond just sex and puppies?

"I need time to think about this," she said, backing up. "Please just give me some time."

"Callie…"

But she didn't wait for him to charm her, touch her and make her forget about everything with his mouth and hands.

She backed up and this time made it out of the club before he could stop her. She hailed a cab. As it pulled away from the curb, her heart clutched at the distressed look on his face. At home, she went to her room and ripped off her clothes, dressed in something comfortable. Knowing this was going to be something she had to do alone, she grabbed a suitcase and filled it with summer clothes and bathing suits. Grabbing the Cabo San Lucas brochure off her nightstand, she clipped the leash on Jack's collar.

"Come on, boy. You're going to have some fun time with Ian." She left her apartment and drove over to Ian's loft.

When she knocked, he opened the door and stepped back. "What's wrong?" he asked, his voice hard.

"I'm going to leave the city for a bit," she said her voice catching.

He reached out and snagged her hoodie and dragged her into the loft along with Jack, who whined softly. He closed the door and pulled her against him. "What's wrong, honey?" his voice now much softer.

She pressed her face to his chest and said, her voice breaking. "Everything is a mess."

The whole thing poured out of her and her big brother, as usual, listened intently. "You talked to Owen? But that only made it worse?"

"Yes, he's talking about committing, and I don't know what I'm more afraid of, if he commits and can't make it work or if it does work."

"Why does that scare you?"

"Because I don't think I fit in his world." Shocked at the words that came out of nowhere, Callie stared at Ian. "I didn't even know I was going to say that. I'm just so not glamorous, a plain Jane. I don't like dressing up that much and I certainly don't think schmoozing with a bunch of people is my thing. Harper's much more suited for that than I am."

"That's not true. But, you're going to do what exactly?"

"I'm going to Cabo to cliff dive. I need to get out of the city and clear my head."

"Cliff diving. Most women I know cry on their couch, paint their nails with their friends, and eat ice cream."

She sniffed. "What are you saying? I'm weird."

He grabbed her around the neck and hugged her close, kissing the top of her head. "You're amazing, Callie. You always have been."

"So you'll take care of Jack for me?"

"Sure. How long are you going to be gone?"

"I don't know, probably a week."

"If I didn't have this show, I'd have Mom come get Jack and I'd go with you. Some sun and fun—"

"And cliff diving?"

"Ah, no. Probably not for me. You're braver than I am."

She laughed through her misery and tears. "Come for a few days then. We could have some brother/sister time."

He shook his head. "Are you sure about that?"

"Yes. Come with me, Ian."

"All right. Let me call Mom and pack a bag. It won't take long." He pulled out his cell and headed for his room, but he turned around. Walking backwards he sent the call and said, "I'm not painting your nails, but I'm so up for crying and ice cream."

She threw a pillow at him. She called her friends and let them know what was going on and they were all sympathetic, especially Brooke. She then called her manager to have her take over the training sessions Callie would miss. Finally, she looked at Jack. He gave her a mournful sigh. "Don't look so sad. I'll be back. You'll get to play in the sun and be outdoors all week. Fresh air and companionship." She reached out and ruffled his fur. But then she wrapped her arms around his neck and buried her face in his fur. "What am I going to do, Jack?" she whispered.

She was still asking herself that when she landed in Cabo and her and Ian went to their hotel. As the shuttle entered through the street-level gates, they pulled up to the orange stucco building, the hotel a large sprawling cliffside resort with panoramic views of the sea, the bay, and rugged mountains. It was located at Land's End rock formation. Callie could only hope that the beauty of the place would give her the peace she needed to untangle this mess in her head regarding Owen.

"Welcome," the bell boy said as he helped her with her luggage. "I'm Pablo and I'm here to make your vacation the best it can be." He was a tall, lanky guy about her age, but he had a smile that could light up the night. Callie smiled back at him as he took care of their luggage. They entered the expansive lobby with high white walls and windows everywhere. They went to the desk and checked in. Getting separate ocean view rooms, it was early, the sun was just coming up over the ocean and the marina to the east.

Unable to access their room until early afternoon, they headed down to the pool area where they found amazing beds near poolside. There was no one around at this time of day and the vinyl beds fully equipped with comfy pillows would do. She lay on her side to get the best view of the ocean. The breeze was warm, but she kept on her hoodie and sweat pants so as not to get cold.

"You doing all right?" Ian asked.

"For now. I'm just tired."

"Get some sleep."

She closed her eyes, but all she could see was Owen's handsome face and the hurt she had put in his eyes. It was ironic that he was the one who wanted to go beyond the boundaries of his comfort zone. She was the one who had just discovered that it hadn't only been Owen's bad boy status, but the fact that his lifestyle was so vastly different from her own, and it was her own comfort zone that was being tested.

Did she fit in? Did she want to fit in? Or, was she afraid that Owen would be the man who could hurt her the worst she'd ever been hurt?

Owen had gone to Callie's loft, but no amount of knocking had brought her to the door. He hadn't slept and it was early morning. He knew it looked a bit desperate that he'd shown up at Harper's penthouse suite, but other than her business phone, he had no personal contact number for Callie. He kicked himself for not getting her number now. He thought about contacting her brother, but Ian wouldn't be forthcoming with information about his sister if she didn't want to talk to him. But he was determined to find her and work this situation out with her before she spooked completely.

The thought of losing her before he'd even had the chance to make something with her spurred him on. She was different from any woman he'd ever met and he wasn't going to let her go without a fight.

He pressed the intercom button and a woman answered with a distinctive Hispanic accent. "May I help you?"

"Yes," he said, trying to calm his breathing. "I'd like to speak with Ms. Sinclair."

"It's very early, sir. Who is calling?"

"Owen McKay. I know it's early, and I apologize, but this can't wait. It's urgent."

He waited with tense anticipation until the elevator opened. He got inside with a relieved breath. As soon as the doors opened, he came out into a hallway that led to her door. Once he knocked, a woman opened the door and ushered him into the foyer. She said, "If you'll have a seat, she'll be right with you."

He was so agitated the panoramic view of New York City was lost on him. The expensive room just a blur as he ignored the white couch and paced.

Ten minutes later, Harper in a sumptuous sheer pink robe over a long nightgown in the same color, the sleeves and bottom trimmed with fine feathers, her hair haphazardly pinned up on top of her head sauntered in. The woman who had let him inside right behind her. "Juliana, coffee please."

"Yes, Ms. Sinclair." The woman disappeared, and Harper yawned, covering her mouth. "Owen, it is way too early in the morning to be so energetic. Please sit down."

He ran his hand through his hair and complied, settling onto the cushions. Harper went to the window and looked out at the city her back to him.

"What brings you here so early?" she murmured.

"Callie."

She turned around, leaned against the window and folded her arms. That wasn't a good sign. He knew he was taking a chance coming here asking for help from her most formidable friend, but he had to find her.

Harper's slim, elegant brows rose and she asked, "What about her?"

He stood, and she pushed off the window. Before he could say anything, the maid came back with a tray, stopping his words. Harper crossed the room and sat down on the opposite sofa in a flurry of silk and feathers like some elegant flamingo. Without any reason to be standing, he sat down again. Juliana set the delicate china coffee pot, cups, cream, and sugar down on the table between them.

She reached for the pot, poured a cup and handed it to him looking like a regal vintage Hollywood actress. He just stared at her holding the cup until the maid left, then he set it down on the coffee table, the dark liquid steaming, sloshing over the rim and collecting into the saucer.

"I need your help." At her closed expression, he held up his hand before she could speak. "I know this is asking a lot, but something happened—"

"—last night to make her want to get out of the city?"

"Out of the city?" He sat back. Damn, she hadn't just run to a friend. She'd left New York City. Did she really need to get away from him that badly? His heart tightened, knowing that he had to speak with her, make this better somehow. "No, not last night. This has been happening with her since I met her. I can't stop thinking about her, knowing I'm not the kind of man she deserves." Harper went to speak again. "I know, Harper. I know who I was in the past. But, she's...different and I find that I can't just sit idle while she's upset. I must speak to her...today. Where is she?"

Harper looked away as if she was forming her response carefully. "I don't think that telling you where she is would be something she wants me to do."

Owen bit back a curse, his hands closing into fists. "I have no intentions of hurting her further. I just want to talk to her about the situation."

"What exactly is the situation?"

Owen's jaw tightened. "That's private between us," he said flatly.

She adjusted the pink satin bow at her waist. "I'm going to need more than that. I want what's best for Callie. I haven't quite decided if I think you're it." She tilted her head and bit her lip. "But she's smitten with you, too. The both of you have been so hellbent on staying away from each other without much success."

He went to open his mouth, but it was her turn to stop him. She raised her hand, the feathers floating around the wide-open sleeve. "With that being said, I know if Callie wasn't invested in this in some way, she wouldn't have left the city so abruptly. I'm a

155

believer in hitting things directly. I think you are, too. I will tell you where she went on one condition." Her tone was ominous and he wasn't sure what she was going to say, but he was willing to do anything at this point.

"Name it," he bit out.

CHAPTER ELEVEN

HARPER GAVE him a soft smile. "You really are in deep, aren't you?"

"Someday, I hope you can know what this is like, feeling it for the first time as if you're innocent again." After the kind of past he'd had, one he had never wanted to really explain to Callie, he'd closed down so hard, even with his great aunt. It was easier that way and the lifestyle of a club owner worked with his bachelor mindset. If he never got close to a woman, he wouldn't have to spill about who he had been…was… It was an awful secret he harbored. But he wasn't that man anymore and it was easy to dismiss his past as if it wasn't a part of him. She wouldn't have to know anything, he'd just wipe the slate clean. "She makes me want to change because she sees something worthy in me. What is the freaking condition?"

"That you respect her feelings and wishes. Stop pushing if this is too much for her. Give her some space and be patient. Callie is a very balanced person and she's so giving and sweet. That's why I was so tough on you, but Owen, if you've changed, then you deserve to find out where you can go together as long as Callie is secure in what she wants. Is that something you can live with?"

He closed his eyes, the fear loosening its strangle hold in his chest. When he opened his eyes, gratitude in his voice, he said, "Yes, I can live with that as long I get a chance to talk to her. Maybe make this process less stressful."

"I think I can live with that, too." He rose and he headed for the door. "She went to Cabo San Lucas." She told him the hotel, and he was already making plans in his head to catch the next flight out of JFK.

The next thing he knew, he was wrapping Manhattan's Darling, the tough as nails party girl in his arms and hugging her tight. And, she was hugging him back.

When they separated, she said with that hard edge. "If you hurt her, all bets are off."

He nodded. "It's the furthest thing from my mind."

"Good."

It was a whirlwind of activity for him to head home, secure someone to take care of Jill and handle the club, Celeste offered to do both and pack a bag. He didn't get to JFK until four and holding onto his patience as he made his way through security, the line moving at a snail's pace. He grabbed a cup of coffee before heeding the boarding call the minute he stepped to his gate. Settling into first class, he was impatient for the six-hour flight to Cabo. But at the end would be Callie. He'd stop being an idiot and lay it all on the line. Callie needed that, needed to know he was in this one hundred percent.

Callie stood at the balcony and watched as several whales breached the surface and splashed down into the turquoise water, the breeze blowing across her skin. She was glad she'd chosen this oceanfront room. It had a king-sized bed, a jacuzzi tub situated so that she could recline in it and see the ocean from the window. The room was beautiful with its tiled floors, light wooden décor and crisp white color palette. But none of those things, including the view tamed the turmoil churning inside her.

Now that she'd had some sleep and time to think a little, she was feeling a bit of a drama queen for leaving Owen like that. From an early age, she'd prefer to spend her time with the dogs, climbing trees, doing things that tomboys enjoyed. She'd grown up with the loving support of her family, so when she'd moved to the city and was exposed to the glamorous side of it, she pretty much shunned it with her own unique sense of sporty style. But Owen lived in the limelight, his club was all about cutting edge people and their celebrity. She had no interest in any of that. But it was his life. Could she, a plain Jane really fit in there? The answer to that question got tied up in her attraction to Owen.

It would have been easier if she'd realized this problem earlier, but she was so consumed with his bad boy status and his commitment phobic tendencies until he said he wanted to overcome them.

Where had she thought this was going? Maybe deep down she believed he would get tired of her and leave her with a broken heart? Maybe that was still a possibility?

She leaned her head on the wrought iron rail and sighed, scrunching up her face. Maybe she was worrying about all this when she really didn't have to. Projecting wasn't the best course of action.

She should have just stayed in New York City and talked to him. Maybe that was what she needed to figure this all out. Clear communication between them instead of giving into her fears and bolting.

She rose and looked back out at the ocean, the whales, finished with their display, were floating peacefully on the surface. This was the bottom line. If she couldn't get past her own insecurities, she would never open up her horizons and step out of her comfort zone. She'd forever be that uncertain plain Jane forever. Owen had really opened up her sexual horizons. He would be a hard act to follow. It was as if they...connected. Maybe that was the scariest thought of all. To be so connected to him, have these doubts about herself, worry about fitting in. It was enough to make anyone uncertain and to bolt.

The knock on her door pulled her reluctantly away from the whales and her self-discovery. Ian stood there. "You ready for some breakfast?"

"Yes," she said, grabbing her bag that had a change of clothes, her bathing suit, beach cover up and sunscreen.

They went down to the hotel restaurant that had a lovely buffet spread. "I know it's only been a short period of time, but how are you doing after a little sleep and some soul-searching?"

She filled her plate with a bran muffin, fruit, and some scrambled eggs. "Kind of feeling like a drama queen." Admitting it to Ian made her feel marginally better.

"Ah, sis, cut yourself some slack. A new relationship can be daunting, especially with a guy who is a lot like me."

"That's just the thing. He wants to try this with me, commitment. That's a big step."

"Are you worried he doesn't have it in him?"

"I guess a little. It's one thing to say it, but follow-through. You've been to his club. It's wall-to-wall beautiful, glamourous women every night."

"I'm no expert, but when a guy finds the right person, some things don't matter as much."

"Maybe. You're a confirmed bachelor, so you don't know what I mean."

"Probably, but I think you should give him a chance if that's what you want to do. Everyone deserves a chance."

"But you warned me away from him."

"I know, but he's making an effort. That counts for something. But, of course, it's up to you. Ultimately, it's going to be you who has to deal with whatever comes out of it."

She looked at him. Her brother was always there for her. He had given her business advice, helped her with opening Sit Happens and gave her a ridiculously low rent on her loft, but he'd never really offered her romantic advice. He'd teased her, of course, that's what brothers did, but this grown-up talk about what she should do was helping so much. "That's good advice, Ian. I'll think about that."

He smiled. "Let's go have some fun and get your mind off this for a few hours. We're in paradise. Let's act like it."

She nodded. They rented paddle boards and did some vigorous paddling around the area, found a place to stop and have some lunch, then went back to the paddling. The afternoon was filled with surfing and seeing which one of them could ride the larger wave. Ian was a bit rusty, but that man had a God given athletic talent and could easily pick it up again. By the end of the day, they'd had enough of the surf. She had to admit that the physical activity, Ian's antics, and the beauty of the area had taken her mind off Owen for a bit. But now that she was dressing for dinner and, at Ian's insistence, a night of rollicking good fun, she was thinking about Owen again. She went to pull her hair back into her usual ponytail, but then paused, remembering how much Owen seemed to like running his hands through it. She left it down.

Dinner was sedate and the food was good, but she didn't have much of an appetite even after all that activity, but she ate her seafood.

"You doing all right over there?" She looked up to her brother's concerned eyes. "You're quiet. If you're not jabbering, then it means you're thinking too hard."

"I'm sorry, not a very good dinner companion tonight."

"You tired? Can't keep up with me?" She straightened and was about to tell him she could keep up with him on her worse day when he grinned. "I knew that would get you. You're so competitive."

"Jerk," she said, throwing a roll at him. He caught it and buttered it. "We could forgo some dancing, fending off people we aren't interested in and watching drunks make fools of themselves for a sedate night in your room driving yourself crazy. It's up to you."

"You could paint my nails, and I could brush your hair."

He laughed and she joined in. "Ah, no."

"All right. Let's get this party train going then."

They hit the strip and bars with names like Mango Deck, Nowhere Bar, Pink Kitty, and The Giggling Marlin. She found willing dance partners at each place, drinking moderately while Ian did the same. They weren't college kids anymore, and Callie didn't relish a hangover the next day, so she kept up her water intake along with the delicious fruity drinks and excellent tequila. By the time they made it back to the hotel, it was late.

"Let's check out the nightclub."

Not wanting to be alone in her room with her thoughts until she was completely exhausted, she agreed. They entered the place and it was rocking. With a twinge, she realized with the lights and music, the dance floor crowded with people reminded her much too much of FLASH only with less sophistication. After one drink, she was ready to crash. But just as she leaned over to talk to Ian, she discovered he was occupied in a booth with a hottie blonde who was hanging on his every word. *My handsome brother.* She sighed. Maybe one day he would find someone that he couldn't live without. This beach bunny didn't look like forever material, but then, Ian wasn't looking for that. She had to wonder why; they had such amazing role models. But, their parents were a hard act to follow and being in her late twenties, she was wondering if she would find what they had, if Owen could truly overcome his adversity to commitment.

She slipped off the barstool, caught his attention and pantomimed with her thumb that she was heading up to her room. He nodded, the woman was sitting very close to him, and she thought her brother would probably score tonight.

"Hey, honey, you're not leaving yet. Are you?"

She turned to the man who had unceremoniously grabbed her arm. Trying to extricate his grip, she gave him an apologetic smile and nodded. "I am."

As she went to turn away again, he grabbed her again. He was middle-aged, obviously looking for a hook-up the way he was perusing her body. He leaned in and said, "Let's dance and get another round on me. Then we'll see where the night leads us."

"No thank you," she said trying to get him to let him go, but he had a good grip. She turned to search for Ian, but he was preoccupied. Turning back, she jerked to loosen his grip, but that had the effect of causing him to lose his footing because he was drunk. He slammed into her and knocked her up against the bar.

For a moment she struggled with his weight, then it was gone. "Keep your hands to yourself, pal."

That deep, mesmerizing voice. She blinked a couple of times almost feeling disoriented. "Owen?"

He glanced at her, his eyes dark and a stormy blue, a protective light in them so fierce, it made her gut clench. Then he transferred his attention to the drunk. "You mind your own business, *pal.*" The guy said, poking Owen in the chest.

"I didn't come all this way to have a fight with you," Owen said. How had she not noticed how broad his shoulders were or how tall he was, her stomach giving a funny little lurch when she realized how imposing he was being right now. There was something deceptively casual about his stance, one that robbed her of breath, made her feel completely safe and the male aggression in him out there to see. Gone was that cosmopolitan guy, in his place stood the street fighter, the man who had grown up under the worst possible conditions and had made such a success of himself. Her admiration climbed even higher seeing him in this light, knowing that he didn't want to talk about his past only made him even more mysterious and sexy.

"We're leaving together. I don't want any more problems from you. She's spoken for."

The guy put his hands up, backing away at once. Through his drunken haze, he saw how serious Owen was.

"Callie," Ian said, next to her shoulder, eyeing Owen with just as much protective macho attitude Owen had just displayed with her. "Are you all right?"

"I'm fine, Ian." Reassuring him with her eyes and a slight smile. Ian got the message and nodded, backing off.

Owen, taking that as his cue, slipped his hand into hers and started walking. His confidence, his calm way of handling this situation and her seeing him in this light made her realize that this was a man she wanted to get to know better, the kind of man that was worthy of her attention, the kind of man she'd been searching for so long.

They simply walked away from the belligerent drunk and out the back door onto the patio. He didn't stop moving until they were on the sand. The ocean waves crashed, the roar of breaking waves picking up in tempo as the tide rolled in.

He stopped walking and turned to face her. A wave of liquid heat washed through her as her gaze strayed to the sexy curve of his lower lip, and she remembered the feel and taste of his mouth on hers. He just stared into her eyes for a minute, his full of raw emotion, knotting up her insides.

It was when she realized fully how badly she could hurt him, how unsure he was of her, how little he expected for himself. Angry at whomever had done this to him, knowing that her encouragement and attention would help. He'd lost the one person in his life that had cared about him. He was still grieving her. Still finding his way in a world that had left him without support or family. She had so much love in her life. She'd had Ian to run to, Brooke, Harper, or Poe. Her parents would have coddled her, given her sympathy and helped her. But Owen had no one and that broke her heart.

To show her that much after he had been so guarded, she felt like such an idiot for her actions. For the first time since she started down this road with him, she felt as if she could let her guard down, too.

"I'm sorry," she whispered.

He opened his mouth to speak, but she clasped his face in her hands and pressed her mouth against his. It was a compelling need to connect to him after what she'd witnessed, the fact that he'd flown all the way here to find her, the fact that he wanted to talk instead of berating her. All of it filled up her chest until she just couldn't wait another moment to not only be in his presence, but join with him in the physical sense. Mouth to mouth, body to body, flesh to flesh. It was the only way she could take her next breath.

His mouth stopped moving, but still on hers. His forehead resting against hers, they both drew in unsteady breaths. "Callie," he whispered. Then his lips claimed hers, pliant and moist and tasting exquisitely of Owen.

Callie felt the need in him, the lonely, lonely need, and she put her heart and soul into that kiss, wordlessly telling him things she couldn't say out loud. A shudder coursed through him, and he drew a ragged breath, catching her by the back of the head, his jaw flexing beneath her hand as he responded. He moved his mouth slowly against hers, tasting her, savoring her, drawing her breath from her and leaving her weak.

She tangled her hands in his hair, gripping him tight as if he was suddenly going to disappear and she'd wake up in this paradise with a hole in her heart.

Owen deepened the kiss appeasing the ache in her for his response, but making her still want more. She tumbled head over heels with a dizzy spiraling fall, hanging tight to Owen to ground her. Then she was on her back with no roof but a sky full of pinpricks of silver light dotting a velvet black ribbon of sky, the moon a sliver of brilliance. The white vinyl mattress sinking with Owen's weight, he reached up and pulled the curtains, giving them privacy on the deserted beach. Callie rose, reaching for the buttons of his shirt, undoing them to get to his warm, muscled chest. He only tolerated a few moments of her caresses.

Impatiently, he covered her body, the sound of the ocean so close, booming with the beat of her heart. The feel of him hard and hot between her legs, pressed against her core, the fabric of his pants smooth against her bare thighs.

He traced his tongue across her bottom lip, then slipped inside, probing, exploring. He ran his hands over her body, chasing shivers, setting off new ones, sliding lower. Desire swelled inside her, pushing sanity out so madness could claim her. She arched against him, losing herself in his texture, scent, touch. His hands slipped lower, massaging her hips, kneading her buttocks. He snagged the hem of her dress and dragged it up, his knuckles brushing over firm muscles, stroking along the sides of her ribcage.

Beneath the little black dress was nothing but a strip of a black lace thong. He made a soft sound, his mouth capturing her nipple, his tongue rasping over the engorged nub, his teeth enflaming her, his lips tugging. The sensation was incredible, setting off that madness into something wild.

"Owen," she clutched him. "Please." Lifting her hips against his belly, seeking contact, seeking the erection she could feel beneath his fly. But he stayed tantalizingly buttoned up. He moved over her, his mouth found hers as he kissed her hungrily. Breaking the kiss, he murmured, "You're so beautiful, Callie. So freaking beautiful."

His hand touched her stomach, and he skimmed it down to the waistband of her thong, then delved beneath. Her legs spread to give him access, and she gasped when he eased two fingers into her, finding the sensitive bud of her core with his thumb and making her mindless. His mouth found her breast again, hot, wet, and relentless. Callie came with a low sound.

He worked his fly, and she sat up to help him, pressing open mouthed kisses against his smooth chest while he sheathed himself with protection. He pushed her back on the cushion, and guided himself inside, squeezing his eyes shut as he eased into her.

"Callie," he groaned, pushing his face into her throat while his hips moved. She wrapped her arms around him. He murmured hot, sexy words to her as they moved as one. The pleasure built and intensified, swelling inside her until she could barely breathe for the pressure of it.

He found her mouth, his kisses consuming, growing more urgent, more carnal, his thrusts deeper, driving, straining, filling her to bursting. Something hot and intense gripped them, sizzling between them as if the very air was on fire, the booming and rush of the ocean pulsing through her while Owen pumped, then he touched her sending her over the edge and he followed.

They lay there in each other's arms and Callie felt shattered, replete. It was as if she couldn't hear anything but Owen's heavy breathing, the beat of his heart, the sound of her own crashing and falling. Then the surf permeated her hearing and his arms went around her. "Are you cold?"

She didn't realize she was shivering, but it was nothing but aftershocks from their lovemaking. She shook her head and he gathered her close. "You're shaking."

His body was warm and comforting. "Reaction to you being here with me. It was wonderful, and I'm not cold."

With a little hitch in his voice, he said, "This isn't exactly what I was planning to do."

"No?" She dropped her head to look into his face with a wry smile on her mouth.

He studied her, then he chuckled softly, an intimate gleam in his eyes. "Not at first. I wanted to talk to you. You're the one who ambushed me."

"I know," she said her voice husky. "I saw it in your eyes that's why I ambushed you." He kissed her forehead, rubbing his mouth against her hairline. With his eyes closed, he murmured between tiny kisses, "You apologized and swept my feet out from under me. You do that a lot."

She kissed his jaw. "You were so commanding, so confident and in charge in the nightclub. I realized how stupid I was to just leave without talking to you. That's what I'm sorry about the most, that I hurt you."

He shrugged, "You gave me a little taste of my own medicine and you were honest. You have doubts. I won't hold it against you. I understand how you feel. This is new to me, too. We're bound to be confused."

"You came all this way to find me." Her throat closed with a fierce ache as she looked at him, dread seeping in and twisting her insides. They might not be able to keep their hands off each other, but there were still kinks in this relationship that had to be worked out. Big ones.

"I had to." She turned her face into the soft skin of his neck, swallowing hard against the sudden lump in her throat.

"Who ratted me out?"

He caressed her face with the back of his hand, his voice husky when he answered. "That's not important."

"It wasn't Brooke because, well, she'd protect me. It could have been Poe; she has such a soft, romantic heart. But my money is on Harper. She must matchmake. It's in her DNA."

"I think I'm protected by snitch, confidant privileges.

She narrowed her eyes. "Okay, I'll let it go since I'm very glad you're here." She rose up and kissed his mouth, framing his face in both her hands. He kissed her back, cupping her head.

He pulled her down against him and she wrapped her arms around his neck. "Why did you come all this way?"

"I can't stop thinking about you," his voice the softest she'd ever heard. She lay against him perfectly still, something sweet and warm opening up in her and spreading. "I meant it when I said I wanted commitment, exclusivity. I want to make you happy, not upset or worried. I didn't want another day to go by and have you troubled because of how you feel about my lifestyle." He hesitated, then said, his tone gruff, "I didn't like you being gone."

She settled her leg over his. "I don't want to go into this with my eyes closed. I've always been pretty casual, don't really like crowds that much, and prefer my jeans to any dress and heels."

"I live the club lifestyle because I've been a bachelor for so long. Doesn't mean things can't change, but, babe, it is my livelihood."

"I know. I get that. I just don't know if that will work. I'm just trying to be honest. Obviously, we have this crazy chemistry, and I wonder if we can overcome the other stuff."

"Like your friends believe what's written about me? Think I'm bad news and the wrong choice for you. Be honest about that."

CHAPTER TWELVE

OWEN REALIZED this was a big sticking point. He was vulnerable here, opening himself up like this, giving his all to Callie whom he felt right with, so right it was as if something clicked into place. Making the extra effort to show her friends that they had nothing to worry about was an easy task. "They don't really know me. Once they realize how I treat you, they'll change their minds. Don't you think?"

"They're completely reasonable. Brooke's worried about me. That's what she does. Takes care of people. I still feel guilty about ruining her birthday."

"Why don't you just invite them down here, now and we'll spend a few days getting to know each other. I'll treat them, so there's no cost to them."

Callie's mouth dropped open as she scrambled for some kind of response. "Owen, really? You'd do that for me?"

He rose up, his body aligned along hers, the warmth of his skin reflected in his eyes. "Yes, if it'll ease your anxiety and Brooke's. I've already talked to Harper…shoot."

"It *was* her. I knew it." She reached up and slipped her arm around his neck. "Don't worry, I'm kind of glad she did let you know where I was."

"Good. She told me that if I hurt you she'd rip out my heart and feed to the crows."

"Oh, that's pretty violent."

"That's how much she cares about you. I get it. You guys are tight. I don't really have that kind of relationship with men, and definitely not women."

The compassion in her eyes rolled over him. He wasn't accustomed to this at all, especially this. Keeping himself separate and guarded had worked too well. "I pushed everyone away, anyone who tried to get too close, including my great aunt."

Callie snuggled closer, her eyes open and direct, clearly listening to him, supporting him, her fingers caressing his jaw.

His regret was poignant.

But, as he lay there with Callie, he realized something. "My great aunt's love influenced me anyway. She taught me about being wanted, about safety and responsibility. She gave me all the tools I needed." His voice broke. Especially the ones he needed to woo this beautiful woman as long as he kept his head on straight and his fear in check. "Old habits die hard, habits that were ingrained for years on the streets. Don't trust anyone, don't give an inch, never let them see you weak, and never, ever drop your guard." He'd been a warrior child, watching his own back. Lost to the civilized world, a world he'd never really known to begin with. "I lived on the fringes of society, a predator when I could manage it, a scavenger most of the time, and so lost and alone." The acute pain from all those feelings still twisted him up inside. He'd been abandoned, but his great aunt had saved him from not only the streets and its exacting code, but from himself. His voice husky and a whole lot unsteady when he continued. "She saved, me, Callie, truly. I'd give anything...*anything* to get one moment with her to tell her what she has done for me. I thought I'd have more time, but it slipped away. I can only pray that she knew how I felt." His throat was tight and his eyes burned. He rubbed them.

The wily old bird probably knew all too well, better than him. It was too bad for him that he'd discovered this all too late.

"That's why she left you Jill." She wiped at her eyes and his heart rolled over. "I didn't know, Owen. I could only guess. Thank you for sharing that with me." Her voice was so full of compassion, her tone telling him she realized how raw and stripped he was feeling.

"I've never told another living soul about what I just told you." He took an unsteady breath. "It's all I want to say about it, about my past. It's not who I am anymore, and I don't see the point of rehashing it. I want to move forward...with you."

She nodded. "I want that, too, Owen. We'll work on it together."

"You'll call your friends and invite them here? I'll set up all the reservations."

"I'll call them in the morning," she said, her tone quiet. "See if they can get off work on short notice."

He nodded. "That's all you can do." She tightened her arms around him and the comfort he got from that one small gesture was overwhelming.

He nudged her. "So, babe, I presume you have a room here and haven't been sleeping on the beach."

With a sparkle of mischief in her eyes, she said, "They said it was ocean view…how was I supposed to know it was on the ocean."

"Damn, going to the bathroom is going to be interesting."

She laughed softly and reached for her little black dress and thong. He took the scrap of lace out of her hand and slipped it over her feet and she rose to her knees as he drew it all the way up, then snapping the band against her waist.

She gasped, shoved him and he toppled right out of the beach bed onto the sand, completely disheveled, his dick still out. Her peal of laughter came with the billowing of the curtains and his chest felt tight every time the drapes moved and he got a glimpse of her sweet, smiling face and that compact, beautifully formed body.

He rose and parted the curtains as she slipped the dress over her head and did a little shimmy to get it aligned with all those tantalizing curves.

"I could watch you do that over and over again."

"You are such a man," she said, her eyes sparkling. She retrieved her high-heeled sandals by the straps, he put himself back together, and offered her his hand as she moved gracefully onto the sand. She let go and slipped her arm around his waist.

"Let's go to the desk first and get you added to my room."

He cuddled her close and kissed the top of her head. "Let me take care of it for you, Callie."

"I can afford it, Owen."

"I know you can. I bet you can do just about anything you damn well please, but it would give me pleasure to take care of this for all of you. The choice is up to you all."

"All right and thank you."

The room taken care of, the charges now secured with his credit card, they headed for the elevator. Her room was nice with a king-sized bed and a jacuzzi tub facing the balcony. "This is nice. We might have to try this out."

"It seems that I now have much more of an interest in doing that, but right now I am beat. Ian ran me ragged in the waves today, I've been drinking and having illicit sex on the beach. We'll save that for later."

They got ready for bed and settled under the covers. She snuggled against him and slipped her arm around his back, resting her head on his shoulder. Her breath was warm on his neck, and he clenched his jaw, the sensation setting off one hell of a riot inside him. He felt as if he'd just conquered the world.

"I like sleeping this way. Does that work for you?" she murmured drowsily.

He held her sleepy gaze for a moment. "I think this is pretty perfect. I want to hold you for a while."

"It's a win/win then," she said, her lids drifting down over her expressive, green eyes.

He closed his eyes and tightened his arms around her. How was it that holding her felt just like home, when he'd tenaciously fought that feeling and wasn't sure he'd ever known what it felt like? Too stubborn and afraid to let himself have that knowledge, lest it be ripped from him.

But that was it. Holding her felt like home, a warm, sweet, picket fence, flowers in boxes, manicured lawn, home.

He clenched his jaw at just the thought of his luck to have moved in next door to her, their amorous dogs forcing them into each other's orbit. If Jill hadn't gotten pregnant, he might have never pursued her, might have never found…this.

His throat got thick, and he closed his eyes, cradling her tighter against him. He wasn't going to worry about it. He had her now, safe in his arms. He'd deal with everything as it came.

Owen shifted in his sleep. He frowned, breathing in. It was as if someone was…watching him. It was about six, the sun rising and the sound of the ocean calmer than the night before, maybe instead of changing with the tides, it was changing with his moods. And his mood right now was quieter, calmer. It wasn't as if all the doubts went away, that would be unrealistic to think they could be fixed with a little sex and a heart to heart talk. He opened his eyes to find Callie staring at him, a slight besotted smile on her face. He was sure it matched the one he had on his own face right about now. Callie pressed her face into his neck and breathed deep.

"You sniffing me, crazy woman?" he asked, his voice laced with sandpaper.

"Uh-huh. You smell great. You have a problem with that, crazy man?"

"Nope, just checking." He grinned.

"Did you bring running gear?"

"Yes, I did. You want to go for a run on the beach?"

"Yep." She bounded up and was ready to get out of the bed, but Owen snagged her arm. "Just a minute there, speedy."

He jerked her hard and she fell against the length of him, including the impressive hard-on that was a daily occurrence. "Oh, are you thinking of another activity before we hit the beach?"

"I was," he growled. "Two guesses and the first one doesn't count." He rolled over her like a wrecking ball. She giggled and gave herself up to him without any argument.

Sometime afterward, he and Callie got dressed in shorts and T-shirts. She tied up her running shoes. "As soon as I get back to the room, I'll give the girls a call."

He had to admit. He was a bit nervous. He wanted them to at least give him a chance. Really, most of his reputation was manufactured. He could kick himself now, letting the *New York Scoop*, exploit him in their rag to sell drama and gossip. He should have had his head examined. A lot of the articles weren't flattering and it was no wonder that her friends might believe some of those stories. Probably not Harper. She waged her own battle against the same kind of gossip, but in her case, it was a matter of her social status in Manhattan. She did have a reputation to uphold but her party girl portrayal in the *Scoop* undermined her as often as they could get any dirt on her.

"How long you want to run?" she asked. "I could do forty to forty-five minutes."

"That sounds good. I'm starving."

She tossed him a water bottle from the fridge. She tucked her room key in her sock. "Let's go." She slapped him on the butt and raced for the door. "Last one downstairs is a rotten egg."

She went to open the door and ran smack into Ian. He was poised to knock. He laughed and steadied her. "Well that answers my question about how you're doing."

He gave Owen a steady look and he met Ian's gaze head on. He wanted to be with his sister, that wasn't going to change due to any tough brother tactics.

"I'm fine," she said, kissing his cheek. "We're going for a run. You want to go with us?"

"No, I'm…meeting someone downstairs for breakfast. I wanted to check on you first. Invite you if things didn't go well last night or leave you alone if they did."

"Oh, the pretty blonde. I knew she was into you." She punched him in the ribs and he danced back. "Oh, Ian, you're so big and strong. What's the view like from your balcony?" she said in a breathy voice.

Owen laughed out loud at Callie's antics and Ian shook his head. "So, Owen. How is the view from Callie's balcony?"

She gasped and went for him and he backed into a wall while Owen laughed some more. "Pretty damn good," he said, staring at her. She blushed and socked her brother again.

"See you around. Enjoy your breakfast…and your view."

She made a beeline for the stairs and Owen went after her. They pelted down the stairs, him taking two at a time to catch up with her fleeting, slim form. They burst out into the lobby making some heads turn. Owen hot on her heels.

She was barely even breathing hard. "You're the rotten egg," she said with a grin.

Then she turned and froze, staring toward the lobby door. Owen looked in the same direction and froze, too. Brooke Palmer, in a prim, demure flowered sundress, Poe Madigan in a black mini with a white flower and a cross in the center and Harper Sinclair in white linen shorts, a tan silky tank top and a white Panama hat were all standing there gaping at Callie, their bellboy right behind them with their luggage.

She turned around and gave Owen a look full of dread and amusement. "Well, it looks like I don't have to make any phone calls." She lowered her voice. "Do you want to make a run for it?"

As it turned out, he flatly refused to back away from the confrontation, but the three women all were much more interested in pulling Callie outside to the patio. That's where they were now. Owen was sitting a few tables away. As he watched, she was talking a mile a minute. As she did, the women's expressions changed from one of concern, to worry. Brooke was frowning. But he was encouraged that she was here.

Ian sat down next to him and smiled. "Is the big dog in the dog house?"

"Seems that way."

"Aw, they're sweethearts when you get to know them. They have been inseparable since they met. It's tough when the girlfriends aren't on board. It's a deep bond. They probably just want to draw and quarter you."

Owen looked over at Callie's brother who had a smug, satisfied look on his face. Owen picked up his cup and took a sip of coffee. "You having a good time, Mr. Landlord?"

"Yeah, just treat my sister right, pal. Or I'll be looking for a new tenant." He grinned and slapped Owen on the back as he rose.

Ian went over to the table and schmoozed with the three women, and they all greeted him warmly. Then, he met up with the pretty blonde. Taking her hand, he headed down to the beach.

He wasn't about to sit over here like he was in some timeout for much longer. Either they were going to give him a chance or not. And, the only one he was willing to accept was the former.

Just when his patience was at the breaking point, Callie stood and walked over to him. She sat down and said, "I talked to them. I told them my fears and the fact that I wasn't sure about fitting into your lifestyle. I had to be honest that I still have doubts."

He covered her hand as Harper watched him with interest, Poe beamed at him, and Brooke gave him a wary look.

"I wouldn't want you to be any way but honest with them. What's the verdict?"

"They are open to spending time with you because I told them that you mean a lot to me. I told them our friendship is also extremely important and if they wanted me to be happy, they would give you a chance."

"Okay, so far so good. What is the plan now?"

"We're going for our run, and they're going to settle into their rooms, unpack, then meet us for breakfast. Then we're all going down to the beach to relax. Well, they are. I'm going to surf."

"Will you teach me how?"

She gave him a sly glance. "Are you just trying to make time with me, mister?"

"As much as I can get."

"Do you really need me to teach you how to surf?"

"No. I know how, but it would be fun."

She laughed, then sobered. "I do enjoy being with you, no subterfuge required."

He rubbed her shoulders and said, "We'll work it out one day at a time. Okay? No pressure."

She glanced at her friends. "Oh, there's pressure times three."

Owen rose and Callie rose with him. He walked over to the table. All three of them eyed him. "It's good to see you all again. You'll love Cabo. I'll take care of all the expenses, including your rooms." They started to protest, then Callie gave them stern looks.

Harper sat back and smiled. "Thank you, Owen. I've never had anyone pick up the tab. It's nice of you but not necessary."

"It's my pleasure," he said. "We'll see you for breakfast when we get back." He turned away and started down the beach. Callie came after him.

"You really are a confident so and so, aren't you?"

"When I want something, I don't hesitate to go after it. What I want is you." It was his turn to slap her butt. "Now keep up, speedy."

"Oh, you're so going to be beat by a girl."

He laughed as she chased after him.

An hour and a half later, showered and dressed, Owen and Callie headed down to the restaurant. They each filled their plates at the buffet and sat down to enjoy their breakfast. Harper said, digging into her food, "Why don't you tell us about your club and your plans for the future?"

He gave them the history, how he got started and where he was now. As they headed to the beach, Owen said, "I have had success in New York City and Las Vegas and am busy working a deal to open two more clubs. One in Miami and one in LA."

"What do you owe your success to?" Poe asked. "It seems that nightclubs are trendy."

"I started hiring DJs to spin and they are the crowd-pullers and ticket sellers. With social media, a lot of the talent have numerous followers. With the draw of EDM—"

"EDM," Brooke said, then bit her lip. He noticed that she was trying to give him a chance, following the conversation closely.

"Electronic Dance Music."

She nodded and he said, "EDM has really invigorated and energized my club. It's packed on Wednesday and Thursday nights due to the DJ draw, typically slow nights in the club business, but for FLASH, some of the biggest money-maker days. The key is you have to adapt with the times. The lines are long all year for the chance to get into the club with a good-sized cover charge."

"Your success sure shows that you know what you're doing," Poe said. "But won't two new clubs take up more of your time?"

They found some beach chairs and settled down around them, kicking off flipflops and removing cover-ups. He did a doubletake at Poe's leather swimsuit, the top looking like batwings and when she turned around, the back panels covering her fanny matched. Each woman had their own style, but Poe was one interesting woman. "Initially, but only until they're up and running. I will have managers for each of them whom I will work closely with."

"That sounds really exciting. When will you be launching them?" Harper asked.

"I have a party planned a few weeks from now."

"And you took the time to come all the way here to speak to Callie when you're so busy?" Brooke asked, looking impressed.

"Yes." He slipped his arm around her neck, and Callie beamed up at him. "It was worth missing a meeting or two. My backers are probably grumbling, but they know I'm good at what I do, so they'll cut me some slack."

Callie went over to get another umbrella, and he noticed Brooke fidgeting with the lounge chair. He went over an easily adjusted it for her.

"You don't have to bribe me. I'm not impressed by money." She sighed. "But it was a nice gesture."

He looked at her. "It wasn't exactly a bribe. I was the one who caused this mess in the first place with my media profile in the *Scoop*. So, I don't mind paying to have you feel comfortable in getting to know me."

She looked out at the ocean. "So, it wasn't a bribe?" She gave him a skeptical look, but he saw amusement in the corner of her mouth, her eyes giving her away.

"Okay, so maybe a little bit of a bribe."

"Well, it's a good one. It's beautiful here." She folded down to the lounge chair and he sat down crosswise in the one next to her, resting his elbows on his thighs.

She turned her head to look at him. "So, the *Scoop* overdramatized and inflated your profile in their paper?" She toyed with the tie on her blue and white polka dot suit.

He smiled. "Yeah, go figure. A gossip rag makes things up."

"I should have known better then to jump to conclusions about you. I'm willing to give you a fair shake, but, Owen, if you hurt her..."

He nodded. "I have no intentions of hurting her, ever. I promise that."

She nodded.

"Am I trying too hard?"

She sniffed and said, "Maybe, but I think it's...cute."

"But you're not exactly won over yet?"

"Now you're pushing. It's only been a few hours." She closed her eyes, soaking up the sun.

"Right." He rose and walked over to Callie. Poe and Harper were both lounging as well. "You ready for some waves?" Callie asked, looking rested and beautiful in a sporty hot pink and gray one piece bathing suit with a racer back.

"Yeah," he said feeling pretty good about how things were going.

By the third day in Cabo, he was enjoying himself. Destressing in a beautiful environment with four beautiful women was a good way to go about it, even if they were making up their minds about him. And the nights with Callie? They were even better. Before breakfast, he'd called his dog sitter, a trusted tenant in his building. When he sat down to eat, he reassured Callie that Jill was doing great, and she murmured that Jack was having the time of his life with her parents. After they had eaten their fill, Owen suggested that they all go scuba diving.

"I've never been," Brooke said. "Is it hard?"

She had thawed out, but he could still see that she had reservations, and he wanted them all to be cleared up. "No, not at all. It's a unique way to see a whole new world under the surface. You'll love it. Come on, my treat. I know a good group that could take us out. You can't say no."

There was a murmur of agreement around the table, but Brooke was quiet. Poe nudged her. "Come on. It'll be a new adventure. Live a little, sweetie."

Finally, Brooke, looking nervous, agreed.

When they arrived at the shop, Owen held the door for them.

The instructor came out, introduced himself and they filled out the necessary forms. The woman behind the counter then showed them into separate rooms to change into the dive gear while Owen paid for their tour. He'd been scuba diving a lot. Callie was also an expert and he wanted to take her to the Great Barrier Reef. He knew she would love it, but that was for another vacation. He stopped short mentally. He'd never done this before, plan and fantasize on future trips with a woman. He never really thought ahead in a relationship. Surprisingly, it wasn't scary, but felt…good…anticipation making him think about all those days enjoying her exuberant company and all those nights, her passion. He couldn't get enough of her. He slipped into her room as she was pulling the neoprene up over her hips. He slipped his arms around her half naked body and hugged her. "You doing okay, babe?"

"Fantastic," she said, wrapping her arms around his. "Thanks for suggesting this. It'll be a fun adventure with the girls."

"I have a feeling if I'm going to get you for the long haul, I'm going to hear that phrase often."

She turned in his arms and laughed. Gazing up at him, they were silent, just looking into each other's eyes. Finally, he bent his head and kissed her. "What phrase," she murmured.

"With the girls."

"Yeah," she giggled. "We're bonded for life, I'm afraid. We're the dog park babes and don't you forget it."

Fifteen minutes later, after that they boarded the boat, it was a short five-minute ride to the dive site where they were going to explore the underwater beauty of the Cabo San Lucas Marine Park.

It took about twenty-five minutes for the instruction, Brooke looking uneasy the whole time. Owen said, "It can be daunting the first time, but you'll pick it up fast."

"I'm nervous," she said coolly.

The instructor went over the gear, communication, environment and safety. Then it was time to get under the water. The five of them went with the instructor. They weren't disappointed. There was dodging sea lions along with squadrons of mobula rays, bait balls, fish who schooled in one large living, swirling ball. Colorful surgeonfish, and babers, turtles, and a wreck to explore. He hung back, and he could tell Brooke was agitated. When she stopped frozen, Owen swam over to her and grasped her shoulders. He put his hand on his chest and pantomimed that she should breathe with him. Her brown eyes were wide and panicked, but as soon as he gave her reassuring looks and calmed her down, she was fine the rest of the dive and into the next one. He really didn't have to pretend that he liked these women. He didn't just want to win them over just so he could be with Callie. He wanted a genuine relationship with

Callie's friends, something he'd never cultivated before, but they were now important because they were important to her.

By the end of the tour, everyone was ready to get back to the hotel, get some rest, and then enjoy an evening together.

As Owen held the elevator for Brooke, she turned and looked up at him. "Thank you for helping me out. I was feeling a little claustrophobic with that mask and being under the water. You really helped, and I'm grateful." She paused and then leaned up and kissed his cheek. She smiled at him, stepping inside the elevator.

Callie slipped her arm through his as they got out on their floor, her smile bright. "Looks like you did a good job being yourself. You have your chance."

He smiled. He did and he was grateful for that. All he had to do now was make sure he didn't screw it up.

CHAPTER THIRTEEN

IT WAS A WEEK after they had returned to the city, and he hadn't seen much of Callie with their mismatched schedules, the demands of the club and his expansion. Owen stopped by Callie's. He knocked. She opened the door and then lunged at him, wrapping her arms around his neck. "I just got home. Can you have dinner?"

"No, I've got meetings to get to today, so if you want to, you could stop by FLASH later and we'll have dinner in the panoramic room."

She slumped down and made a face. "I'm tired. I wanted to stay in, but I could make the effort."

"No, not if you're tired. I'll try to get off as early as I can. Maybe we can have a late dinner?" She looked so disappointed, he wrapped his arms around her. "Things should calm down once this expansion business is over." She nodded. He slipped his finger under her chin and lifted her head. "I've missed you. Sleep over tonight?"

She brightened. "Yes, that works for me. I don't have a client until eleven tomorrow."

"Then it's a plan. Late dinner and snuggling. We'll see what other trouble we can get into after that."

"Ooh, that sounds naughty. Count me in all the way."

He laughed and kissed her again.

Once he hit the club, he was going pretty much non-stop. Celeste came in with the end of the month reports and he was pleased with the increase in profits. His soon-to-be backers would also.

"Looks good." He said handing them back to her. "How is the announcement party coming along."

"I'm progressing on it, but one of the backers can't attend. He wanted it moved to the next night."

"Is that possible for you to do that with such short notice?"

"I covered for you and your unplanned, impromptu disappearance," she said. Her voice was mild, but when he looked up there was a hardness in her eyes.

He leaned back in his chair. "Do we have a problem here?"

"Only, it would have been nice if you'd consulted me on your trip."

"It was personal and if I'm not mistaken, you work for me."

She smiled sweetly and folded the reports against her chest. "That's right, Owen. I work for you." She turned to go, then turned back. "I forgot to mention. The backers want to have dinner with you one day next week. I thought Monday was a good night since it's slow at the club."

"That will work. Make sure that you put that on the calendar and make a reservation for five."

Her brows rose. "Five? But there's just you and three backers. Did I count wrong." Her eyes lit up. "Unless you wanted me to go along." Her tone was hopeful.

"No, I'm inviting Callie. It's time she met them and got acquainted. We'll be working together for a while."

"Callie? Owen, she's not exactly the best choice. I'd be a better asset at that dinner. I know all the facts and figures. All the information. It's just good business to have me go instead."

"Maybe so. All right, you come, but also include Callie."

Something flashed in her eyes, and she gave him a tight smile and nodded. "All right."

As the night wore on, he tried several times to get away. He texted Callie he was leaving, then something would surface and he'd have to deal with it. It was late when he got off the elevator at home. He knocked on her door, but there was no answer. He didn't want to wake her if she was asleep, but he certainly didn't want to eat and sleep alone.

Grumbling to himself, he headed for his loft. He fit the key in the lock and opened the door. She was sitting at his table. It was set with nice plates and candles burned all over the room, throwing a burnished glow over everything. He smiled when he noticed that she'd even shaped the napkins into little dogs. The breathtaking view of the New York City skyline framed in the window looked picturesque.

But it was the woman at the table he focused on.

"Hi, babe," she said and rose, wearing a lacy tank top and a tight pair of jeans, a sweater was thrown over the back of the sofa. She must have gotten warm while she cooked. "I made you a special dish."

It smelled heavenly in there and when she reached him, she slipped her arms around his waist and turned her face against his neck. Drawing her hips flush to his, resting his jaw against her head as he began slowly massaging the small of her back. Callie sighed.

"You're tired," he whispered.

"So are you," she whispered back. She drew him over to the sofa. Pushing on his shoulders, she made him sit, then she snaked around him and started to knead his back and shoulders. He closed his eyes, her hands strong and firm against his tight muscles. "It smells good, but not as good as you," he growled, snagging her and dragging her onto his lap.

"How was work today?" she said, running her hands through his hair, her eyes caressing his face.

"Hectic. Always seemed to have something cropping up."

"That's interesting. They could do fine without you for almost a week, then it's chaos when you get back. Maybe Celeste wants to keep you there."

He looked down into her face. "I'm not interested in her, Callie," he said flatly. "You believe that, right?"

"Yes, but I think she's still interested in you. You had a relationship with her. You work with her. Maybe she thinks you and I are a temporary thing."

"I had a casual on and off with her and she works for me. In retrospect, it was a stupid thing to do, but—"

"Convenient."

"Does that make me a callous bastard?"

"Maybe a little. You just hadn't discovered what a real relationship could be. You were guarded and wary of committing. It sounds exactly what you would have done. I'm not going to judge you, Owen."

He exhaled and cuddled her closer. "I made it clear to her what we had was over. I needed to be free for you. At the time, I didn't realize it."

"Realize what?"

"That I was making room in my life for you. Celeste is my business manager, nothing else."

Callie tightened her arms around him, and Owen could feel a light quivering in her, as though she was worried. "She's so beautiful, poised, dresses like the women you're used to."

Shifting his hold, he cradled her head firmly against him and brushed a gentling kiss against her temple, his expression disquieted. "You don't have to worry about her. I'm not interested one bit."

She wrapped her arms around his neck and sighed. Owen might be sure that his attention was completely focused on her, but Callie thought the woman had an agenda. Whether he realized it or not, she was still interested in him. It was clear to Callie each and every time they came into contact.

"Oh, before I forget, the announcement meeting has changed to the following evening. Will that work for you?"

"It might cost you," she whispered.

He chuckled and nuzzled her neck. "How much?"

"Plenty."

"I like the sound of that."

"I promised Brooke I'd help at the homeless shelter." She kissed his lips. "What time?"

"Seven."

"That will work perfectly. I can make that and speaking of dinner, we'd better eat before it's inedible." He released her and she scrambled off his lap and went into the kitchen. "It's something my mom makes and I'm sure you'll love it."

"I'm sure I will."

"Chicken, pasta, mozzarella cheese, and a white sauce. Chicken Fettuccini."

She brought the dish over to the table and her heart gave a little squeeze when he smiled at her dog napkins. Settling down they dished up the meal and ate while Owen told her everything that went wrong today.

After they finished, Callie rinsed the dishes while Owen wiped off the table, turned on the lights, and blew out the candles. The scent of green tea leaves and a floral scent she loved lingered. Then he turned on some soft classical music and went to change. She had the dishes in the dishwasher and fresh coffee made by the time he returned. She was standing at the sink, washing the basin and running the garbage disposal, and he came up behind her, reaching for two mugs from the cupboard beside her. His presence washed through her. He didn't touch her, but she could feel the heat from his body, and she braced herself and closed her eyes, sensations sluicing through her, making her body tighten and hum.

Owen poured two cups of coffee, then leaned against the stove, watching her.

Working on keeping herself in check, she lifted her chin toward the fridge. "There's a cheesecake in there with your name on it."

He raised his cup and took a sip, then said, "Sounds perfect. Let's cut a couple of slices, sit down on the sofa and enjoy it."

She reached up for plates, but she felt his arms around her waist, turning her. His eyes were soft and intense. Held transfixed by the intimacy in them and by his touch, she stared at him, her heart jumping into a little faster beat.

He stroked her lip, his voice soft and husky, more seductive. "I forgot something when I got home. I don't deserve any cheesecake."

"What? Why?"

Feeling as if she could drown in those pools of blue, he tilted his head, looking boyish and sexy, so male all at the same time. Gathering her against him, he cupped her jaw, his fingers hooking behind her neck, just under her ear, then he lowered his head and took her mouth in a drugging kiss. The kind that was definitely a "hello" kiss with a capital H. "I loved having you here when I came home," he whispered against her mouth.

She wrapped her arms around him. "I think in this case, I will overlook your transgression and allow you some cheesecake."

"You are a saint."

She rolled her eyes, releasing a heavy, put upon breath. "Don't I know it."

He chuckled and let her go, pulling open the fridge and taking out the container. She held the plates for him as he served up two pieces and replaced the dessert in the fridge.

They sat down, but before she could dig into her treat, he took her hand, brushing her knuckles with his thumb. There was a brief silence; then he raised his head and looked at her something warm and sweet in that gaze. "Once we get this announcement behind us, we should take off for a few days. You deserve a break."

His suggestion caught her off guard, but it was his seriousness that made her feel so giddy and alive inside. He was, right here, right now planning something for the future.

"I would love that," she said softly. She turned her hand and laced her fingers through his, smiling into his eyes.

"You do, too, Owen."

He held her gaze for a moment longer; then he glanced down as he tightened his fingers around hers. "Yeah," he said gruffly. "But, I want to spend time with you."

Then they went to bed. As she lay against him, she marveled at how far they had come since she'd ogled him, thinking he was an untamable bad boy.

He murmured drowsily. "Are you free for dinner on Monday?"

"Why?"

"I'm dining with the backers and they wanted to meet the woman that is rumored to have made me settle down."

"Did I tell you that I hate that I'm showing up in the the *Scoop*."

"It was bound to happen."

"But, I think they delight in finding me at my worst. It seems that I always have to think about how I look every time I leave the house. It's uncomfortable, Owen."

"It'll blow over and they'll be more interested in someone else. We won't be giving them anything to gossip about."

He fell asleep, but Callie couldn't seem to settle the churning in her gut. She knew that getting involved with Owen was going to shove her out of her comfort zone. But the comments in the *Scoop* were just horrible, unflattering, and sometimes downright mean. They had called her dowdy, untidy, someone with absolutely no fashion sense. Which was completely wrong. The tone was incredulous that Owen McKay had settled down with a mousey-haired tomboy who thought sweatshirts made a fashion statement. She just didn't fit in with all those glamourous women he used to hang around.

All her old doubts about this relationship surfaced. Owen's lifestyle really hadn't changed, but she was the one being scrutinized under a fashionable, high-class microscope and she hated it. Maybe he was right and it would subside, but while she was enduring the weekly attacks on her style, it was hurtful.

It wasn't Owen's fault. He wasn't feeding them their lines, he wasn't parading her around and he wasn't encouraging them to make any statement about him at all. If anything, it seemed as if people were more interested in him now that he'd started dating her then when he'd had those stick women with no souls on his arm.

Maybe that was news because she was out of the ordinary. She stuck out from that crowd and it was a known fact gossipers and celebrities were notorious for hoopla. It was dramatic that New York City's premier bachelor had seemingly fallen for someone so far away from what he had dated.

If anything, it made Callie even more attracted to him. He was the fabric for their rag. She really should just let it wash off her back like a duck.

When Monday rolled around, Callie hadn't seen much of Owen. He'd been working hard on the expansion and his announcement party. She understood.

She finished work, walked and fed Jack who was as usual excited to see her. But the moment he was done with loving on her, he was at the door. "Hmmm, I think I've been replaced as your number one, Jackie." He gave her what sounded like a chastising woof and she laughed. "I'm just kidding, you big lug." Owen had given her a key and she remembered how warm and fuzzy that made her feel. She took Jack with her when she went over to check on Jill to feed her, too.

Jill rose a little slowly, her tail wagging when she saw Jack. They nuzzled each other and Callie petted her sleek head. Her tummy was larger now, and she ran her hands over the bulges. Poe had been here just last week and said that she was doing great. Owen was taking excellent care of her and she was in excellent health. He had beamed. After knowing the story about Jill, Callie figured that was all about his great aunt Tilly. Once they finished eating, she took them both for a walk.

She left Jack with Jill as she left Owen's loft. Going back inside hers, she grabbed up her garment bag with her stylish, somewhat boring little black dress, her stylish coat, undergarments, and pricey heels. Harper had helped her pick out the dress. Callie fingered the shiny sports jersey style dress that she picked out herself. When she moved in it and the light caught the ginger sequins, it turned parts of them a tangerine orange, a big white 81 in white on the back. She thought it was so awesome.

She sighed and left it in her closet as she caught a cab downtown to the shelter where Brooke volunteered. She hung the garment bag on a hook in the back and picked up a clean apron. Brooke was already out front in the line. Callie joined her.

"Hey, you made it." They hugged and Callie grabbed a pair of plastic gloves and started setting cornbread onto the plates that passed her by, smiling and greeting the people. She worked up a sweat in the hot area just in front of the kitchen. She'd have to use the restroom to sponge off before she changed.

"How are things going with Owen?"

Callie made a face and Brooke touched her arm. "Is he being a jerk?"

"No. Owen is great—"

"I hear a "but" in the statement."

"I don't see him much and *The Scoop* is really getting on my nerves."

Brooke winced. "I saw the latest. Man, they had no right to call you a bag lady."

"I was walking Jack and I like to be comfortable at the end of the day. Who doesn't?" Mortified, Brooke fumed. "They really said I looked like a bag lady?" Callie raised her voice. "The sweatshirt I was wearing, I bought at an upscale store. It has the logo on it and everything. I'm not a bag lady."

A woman stopped and gave her the evil eye. "No offense," Callie said. The woman snatched the cornbread out of her hand and moved on.

"Yeesh, now I'm insulting homeless people."

"Not intentionally." Brooke slung some mashed potatoes on one of the proffered plates. "We know you're not a bag lady," Brooke whispered, touching her arm. "But it's not about the quality of what you wear. It's that you, according to them, don't measure up. That's what burns my toast."

"Exactly. According to them. I have half a mind to go down to the office and tell them to lay off."

"That won't do any good. They will just recite the first amendment and have security escort you out of the building."

She stared at Brooke for a moment. "You didn't—"

"Go down there and complain?" She huffed a breath. "No, but I wanted to."

"I'm going to this very expensive place tonight."

"Don't forget to exclaim over the wine and use your napkin."

"Check. I won't eat with my feet, but that would be easier than figuring out what utensil to use with what dish."

"I have a tip. I dated a Wall Street guy once. Extremely boring, bad in bed, but he sure knew how to wine and dine. Anyway, watch what he does. That got me through more than one meal."

"Good tip," Callie said, high-fiving her. "I have to look the part even though they never give you enough to eat and they're so pretentious about how it looks on a plate. Itty bitty food, big, honking check."

Brooke laughed and nudged her with her shoulder. "Just have some ice cream when you get home. That's a good excuse."

Callie flushed, nodding, the humiliation making her squirm. To think so many people read that damn paper and clucked their teeth and shook their heads, thinking how Owen had fallen. As the hour wound down, and it was time for her to leave for the restaurant, Callie removed her apron and said goodbye to Brooke. She pulled out her cell to text Owen.

In mid-text, she turned and looked up when she heard angry voices. With only one piece of cornbread left, three men started shoving each other. One hit the table and dislodged a wooden spoon that cartwheeled up and then down on a bowl of blueberry sauce. The topping jumped into the air, purple spattering all over Callie's shirt. She lost the grip on her cell, and it flew into a pot of gravy. She watched horrified as it sank out of sight.

She gasped at the wet, heavy stain and turned to give Brooke an open-mouthed gape. The three men looked chagrined and the lady who had been within hearing distance of her "bag lady" comment, grinned.

Luckily, she could wash up and change. But her cell was a goner as one of the helpers fished it out of the pot with a metal ladle and dropped it on a towel.

"You can wear mine," Brooke said, her shocked eyes meeting Callie's.

"I don't know Owen's number by heart."

Brooke, who had gotten some of the sauce on her shirt as well, steered Callie to the back. But when she walked over to the place where she'd hung her garment bag, it was gone.

She stood there for a moment, feeling as though she had just been launched into a bad dream. Frantically she turned to the people who were in the kitchen. "Did anyone see my bag?"

All she got were people shaking their heads. "Oh my God, I've got dinner with Owen in half an hour. I have just enough time to change and get over there. What am I going to do? Someone stole my clothes and shoes."

"We could go to my apartment."

"I don't have time, and I can't be late."

Brooke grabbed her arm and dragged her into the restroom. "What?" Callie asked as the door closed behind them. Transfixed by shock, she looked at Brooke, her numb reaction turning into dread as it settled like a weighted load of bricks in her stomach.

Brooke pulled her shirt over her head and started to clean the stains dotting it. "You can wear mine." She looked at Callie's huge splatter and said, "It's not as bad as yours."

Suspended by horror, Callie stood rooted to the spot, the only sound penetrating was the sound of the hand dryer. Suddenly cold, she slowly rubbed her upper arms, her gaze riveted to her reflection in the mirror. There was blueberry sauce on her face, in her hair. Her hair was a mess. "But, I'm wearing jeans. I wanted to look my best when I met them. This is a complete disaster."

"You'll bowl them over with your personality. I have no doubt." Brooke said, in nurturing mode as she stripped off Callie's shirt and tugged the now wrinkled, slightly less stained garment over her head. "Let's get that washed off." Grabbing a paper towel, she wiped the blueberry sauce off her cheekbones and cleaned it as best she could out of her hair.

She was going to one of the most expensive restaurants in Manhattan, La-dee-da, for God's sake. Owen had to secure the reservations a week in advance, and pay a fee to hold it. The meal for five people was going to cost three thousand. The cream of Manhattan's society was going to be there dressed to the nines for dinner. She had on a stained, creased shirt, a pair of ratty jeans and scuffed sneakers. Her throat closed up.

All Callie could do was stare at her reflection and make a strangled sound.

CHAPTER FOURTEEN

OWEN LOOKED at his watch for the third time. He was getting worried. Callie was supposed to text him fifteen minutes ago when she was headed over here from the shelter. The three men who sat around the table in La-dee-da had approached him about backing him for two more clubs about a year ago. He'd had turned them down. Owen wasn't sure he wanted two more clubs to manage. The profits would pad an already impressive bank account. But, they had, however, persisted and Celeste had encouraged him to take the deal. They would assume the risk and Owen could cut his losses if it went south. Celeste had been confident it wouldn't. With thoughts of Callie buzzing in his head, he looked at his watch again.

"Is something wrong?" Devon Martin said, frowning.

"It's Callie. She should be here any minute."

Celeste was engaged in conversation with the most persistent of the three, a middle-aged balding man who looked like a weight-lifter, Steven Degrasse. The third backer, Tucker Montrose said, "We would be fine with you giving her a call."

"I think I'll do that." He rose and walked toward the blue front doors and pressed her quick call number. He waited and waited, but it rang right through to voice mail.

"Owen," someone hissed from behind the potted ficus near the door. His head whipped up and he gaped. Callie stepped out from behind the plant dressed in worse for wear jeans, a rumpled, stained and worn top. He strode over to her. "Callie? What's going on? Are you all right?"

She started to explain and her voice got more and more strained and upset as she went through her whole ordeal. As she talked, the tightness in his chest and his worry evaporated. He knew he shouldn't be amused. Knew that she was distraught, but he couldn't help it. It sounded like an *I Love Lucy* episode. He gave her a long, assessing look, trying with all his might to keep the amusement tightly wrapped up, he caught her by the back of the neck and gave her a friendly little shake. "You look fine. We'll just explain what happened."

"Fine? I look like a...a...bag lady."

He had to bite the inside of his cheek. She was so freaking adorable. He just wanted to take her home and make love to her all night. He was caught completely off guard when she leaned back against the wall and covered her eyes with one hand. It was only then that he saw how badly she was shaking.

Calling himself every name in the book, he stared at the ceiling trying to ignore the tight feeling in his chest. He heard her take a ragged breath—a breath that sounded too much like a sob for him to ignore, and with his will evaporating like smoke, he caught her wrist and turned her into his arms. He gathered her against him. "Babe, *babe*," he murmured gruffly. "It's not worth it. It's just a bunch of rich people eating. Who gives a fuck what they think?"

Drawing a trembling breath, she slid her arms under his suit jacket and around his back. "I wanted to make a good first impression, for you."

"You've already made a good first impression on me."

Tucking her head tighter against him, he rubbed the silky disorder of her hair, a flicker of amusement surfacing. "I don't really care about what you're wearing. I like you better naked, every time."

"Oh, that's comforting," she said, her mouth twisting, wiping at her eyes. "I'll cause a stir if I strip and then get arrested for indecent exposure."

He chuckled and she gave him a dirty look. "We can call you a *sac dame*. It sounds better in French." She buried her face against his chest.

He got an unsteady laugh, her voice muffled. "Owen, it *doesn't* sound any better in French."

He waited until he felt her begin to relax; then he eased his hold and lifted her face so he could see her eyes, his expression ruthlessly controlled. "You'll start a whole new fashion trend."

Her golden lashes matted, her mouth not quite steady, she looked at him, hers so dilated there was hardly any color. She stared at him for a moment, then said, her voice husky. "Shabby chic a la blueberry?"

He threw back his head and laughed. "Now you've got it."

She narrowed her eyes and slugged him in the shoulder. "I'm so glad this amuses you. Maybe we should call it *chic délabré a la myrtille?*"

He felt her catch an uneven breath, and he tightened his hold, experiencing such an overwhelming feeling of emotion, it left him breathless. Waiting for it to ease, he slid his hand under her hair, molding the collar of her coat around her neck, then said, allowing a trace of amusement into his voice. "Good one and I will say that phrase *does* sound better in French."

From behind him, he heard Celeste's voice. "What is taking you so long?" she hissed.

Owen stepped away and Celeste got the full view of Callie. Her eyes widened and her mouth fell open. She marched forward, looked at Owen, then back at her. "Oh my God, you can't be serious? This is a classy place and you look like you just rolled out of a rag bag."

"Celeste, drop it."

"Drop it? Owen—"

He turned to her and got in her face. "I said, drop it!" Anger ran through him, tightening his hands and clenching his jaw, so he ground out the words. He wasn't about to have her rude comments make Callie feel any worse.

She snapped her mouth shut and gave him a fuming look. "Fine." She turned on her heel and strode from the entrance.

He got another unsteady laugh, and she tucked her arm through his. "My hero," she murmured as they entered the dining room.

He ignored everyone and the soft murmur that told him people were talking about her attire. He pulled out her chair and seated her. There was complete silence at the table. Celeste looked like she was fit to be tied and the three men just stared at Callie.

"This is my girlfriend, Callie Lassiter. She runs a dog training business called Sit Happens." The men chuckled and Owen continued. "She owns a Great Dane and so do I. When they got loose one day, they mated and we were practically strangers, neighbors, but now we're more." There were smiles on everyone's faces except Celeste's. She scowled and sipped her wine. Then Owen let Callie explain what happened and why she had shown up dressed like she was.

They also got a chuckle out of that, and just like that, she charmed the pants off them. It helped that all three of them were dog owners, and they had a lively discussion about training. Then someone mentioned basketball, and that started off another conversation until the evening wound down.

The party broke up and Owen paid the bill. Celeste had barely spoken three words to him. She left in a huff after saying goodbye to the backers. Owen and Callie exited the restaurant. "Cab?"

"Let's walk for a bit."

He wrapped his arm around her and she clasped his waist. They walked a few blocks and Owen crossed the street and froze. A building loomed in front of them, ramshackle, the doors and windows boarded up. Memories flooded him of dark, dirty times, a combination of terror, hunger, cold, heat and a hollow feeling filled him. His mind twisted away from what he'd had to do to survive, the loathing sucking the heat out of his body, his skin crawling. Callie was speaking, but the memories took him over, and all he wanted to do was run. Get away from what had been his past.

"Owen!" she shouted and he snapped out of it, staring down at her. His mouth went dry. What had he done? He'd opened himself up, vulnerable and bare. He broke away from her. But she stared at him then the building. "What is it?"

His mind racing, the memories still fresh, his reluctance to share any of that ugly truth with her like an iron vice strangling him. He shook, trying to get control. He wasn't that boy anymore. He was a man, successful, moving into a future with a woman he adored...his thoughts scattered...loved. He loved her and he would never, never reveal what he had been.

He found his voice. "This is where I once lived."

"Owen."

"I can't talk about it," he whispered.

Her eyes softened and filled with a compassion that stabbed at his tender heart. She closed the space separating them, threw her arms around his neck and clasped him close, her heat thawing the frozen pain icing his heart. "You don't live here anymore. There's nothing you need to tell me right now. When you're ready, I'll listen. You're not him anymore, Owen. Your great aunt saw to that. Remember what you told me? How she saved you?"

He nodded, the memories of his aunt Tilly feeding him that first night, and he hadn't been able to hold that much food and he'd gotten sick. She'd held his head, cleaned him up, bathed him tenderly without a word, soaping his hair and his thin body. Her face had been open and kind as she'd washed the tears from his flushed cheeks. Then she'd given him clean, soft, good smelling clothes and a warm, comfortable bed to sleep in. Safe. That's what that feeling was when he thought of Aunt Tilly. Just safe. The grief overwhelmed him for a moment, and he clung to Callie, the pain of losing her, crashing over him. "I loved her," he choked out.

"I know, Owen, and she knew it, too. I'm sure of it." She kissed him, wiping gently, tenderly at his cheeks with her thumbs. She raised her arm and yelled, "Taxi!" A yellow cab pulled to the curb. She looked over her shoulder for a moment, jerking with a little shiver. "Someone should do something about that place." She slipped her arm through his. "Come on, babe. Let's go home."

That word filled him up and once inside his loft, she showed him with soft touches, passionate kisses, and warm skin just how much he meant to her, surrendering herself to him until he had all of her inside him. She filled up every inch of him, but it was as if he expanded to hold more, as if there was so much of her, all he could do was grow larger to absorb it. And when he sank into her, when he took her with all that love and passion for her that also seemed to expand, all he could think was...safe.

He was safe with her.

Afterwards, he murmured to her. "I'm starving."

She laughed and smiled "Well I guess La-dee-da wasn't La-dee-enough."

"Hell, no. That pretentious stuff couldn't fill up a squirrel let alone a freaking grown man and woman."

"But the wine was so good," she said with so much sarcasm, he rolled with laughter. When the doorbell rang, she grinned and said, "What did you do?"

"Ordered pizza from Tony's."

"Bless you," she said, peppering kisses all over his face, then she raced to the door. They ate it in bed and fell contentedly to sleep in each other's arms.

In the morning as he drank his coffee and stared out the window toward where that building stood, he thought about what she had said. *Someone should do something about that place.* He pressed his forehead to the glass and closed his eyes. When he'd put up his walls so he wouldn't get hurt again, he'd closed off everything. He'd amassed a fortune, he'd been hedonistic and selfish, thinking only of protecting himself while the misery he'd escaped had endured without him. He thought by shutting it out, he could escape it. A lump formed in his throat and something began to change and grow in him, something that was bigger than himself. Bigger than his plans and much more important than anything he'd ever done in his life before.

Except for Callie. She would always be the exception. He pushed away from the window and left the loft. Once at his office, Celeste informed him that the announcement party was back to the original date. He was preoccupied and he told her to make sure she let Callie know. He sat down at his desk and brought up his financial statement and started to catalog all his assets.

The day before the announcement party Callie went to Poe's to help her paint her bedroom this gorgeous sage green color. She wore her rattiest clothes and pulled her hair into a ponytail, threading it through the back of a ball cap.

Brooke and Harper were already there, but Harper spent her time sitting on the floor and playing with the Terrible Two because trying to contain those animals inside the bathroom would be a study in patience. She sat with them, a pull-rope toy in her hands as they simultaneously growled and attacked it with vigor.

She leaned over and picked up the *New York Scoop* and started to thumb through it, rolling her eyes as pictures of Harper seen with no less than three different men on three separate locations filled the page. "Looks like you're now fodder for that rag. I hate them."

Harper nodded. "With good reason. They have been merciless and horrible to you. I've got the notion to give them a piece of my mind."

"They won't listen," Brooke said.

"Right," Poe replied. "They've got the law on their side, and I'm sure it brings in a lot of money."

"They sure have gotten yours," Harper grumbled.

"Hey, I just want to stay up-to-date on all the goings-on. Who's doing who and whatnot. Sue me. I love the drama."

"Exactly," Brooke said, carefully taping around all the woodwork.

"Poe, do you have any wine?"

"In the fridge, but Harper, I won't be exactly dexterous with alcohol. If you drink on an empty stomach, the alcohol not metabolized by the liver can be detrimental to your brain, especially the parts that handle movement, speech, judgment, and memory."

"Right. We're aware, Poe." Harper got off the bed and said, "Come on you little rascals." They followed her out of the room. "Where are your wine glasses?" Harper shouted.

"Left cupboard, top shelf," Poe shouted back.

Harper came back into the room with the Terrible Two hot on her heels. She had a package of dog treats clamped in her teeth, a wine bottle in one hand and four glasses in the other. "Let's get this painting party started!" she said as she dropped the bag on the bed and used Poe's draped nightstand to set down the glasses. She opened the bottle and poured four drinks. "Come on you guys," she groused. "Drop the brushes."

When everyone complied, because, yeah, who argued with Harper? Ah, no one. Each of them took a glass. She raised hers and said, "To six months with three of the best damn women I have ever met. I think if I have my way..." she winked at them, "...and I usually do. We'll make this for life."

Callie smiled. "I'll drink to that."

Poe said, "I'll ruin a few brain cells for that."

Brooke said, "You're like the sisters I never had."

Harper groaned and glanced at Poe, who said, "Group hug!"

Callie didn't bother cleaning up much at Poe's. She'd head home and get a nice hot shower and then…she was in the mood for pancakes. She'd have breakfast for dinner. Owen would like that, too.

When Callie's cell phone rang, she answered, her voice upbeat. She was feeling great. "Owen is waiting for you," Celeste said, her voice sour and harsh. "You better get over here." Then she hung up.

Perplexed, Callie wasn't sure why Owen would want her at FLASH this time of day. It was two hours before he would open the doors. Shrugging, she figured he probably wanted her to see the set up for the announcement party the next day.

She hailed a cab and was at FLASH in about twenty minutes. She went around to the back and came in through the kitchen entrance since the front doors were most likely locked. She heard music playing, but a softer tone, then she heard voices and she frowned. What the heck?

She pushed open the door and stepped out into the area filled with people dressed up like they were attending…oh holy hell…she looked up to see the banner. It was the announcement party and here she was looking like hell, again.

Celeste sidled up to her. "Really, Callie. Do you think you are the best person for Owen? She opened *The Scoop* and shoved it into her hands. There was a picture of her the night she'd shown up at La-dee-da. Humiliated she read the caption: *Has Ms. Lassiter found the premier place to shop? Is she picking through the leftovers of a homeless shelter to come up with this dismal ensemble. She should have stuck to Goodwill. This folks is bottom of the barrel chic. Ms. Lassiter is in a worst dressed category of her own.*

Owen looked up in time to see a paint spattered Callie holding the *Scoop* in her hands. He frowned. She looked at him, her eyes stricken. Without saying a word, she turned on her heel and left.

The look on her face made him think that she might have just had enough of the spotlight and him. He panicked and stepped away from Devon in mid-sentence. Then his eyes cut to Celeste. Adrenaline spurted into his bloodstream when he saw the smug, satisfied look on her face. Then it hit him. He'd told her to make sure Callie was aware of the change in the date. But it was clear to him that she hadn't. She'd set her up to look like a fool.

He swore savagely, so damned mad he could barely see straight. When he reached her, he grabbed her arm and hauled her behind the bar.

"What did you do?" His voice filled with disgust.

Celeste lifted her chin. "Nothing. I don't have to do anything for her to look like an idiot. Surely you have to see that."

He gave her a caustic stare. "You're lying and conniving. I thought I made myself perfectly clear when we spoke. I'm never going to be with you ever again. I'm in love with her and you might have ruined everything with your interference. Get out, clean out your desk and fucking get out of my club. You're fired."

She sputtered her eyes widening. Her face ashen. He turned to leave, but she grabbed his sleeve. "I can't believe you're doing this to me after everything I've done for you. Owen, please," she said, desperation in her voice.

He jerked his sleeve out of her grasp, his tone cold and cutting. "I didn't do this. You did. I don't want to see you again."

"You won't, but I demand severance and a recommendation. This has nothing to do with my skills or abilities."

His mouth tightened, and he wanted to roar, but even though he was pissed off about what she had done to Callie, he couldn't argue with her. "Done. Now leave."

The music had drowned out their conversation, but the moment he stepped toward the front door, Devon caught his arm and drew him into conversation. He thought about just blowing everything off, but he figured Callie would need some time to cool off. He wasn't going to let her go no matter what she said. He just had to get through this, then he was packing her up and taking her to Australia for opera, the Outback, the rainforest, and scuba diving in The Great Barrier Reef. He was going to make love with her and tell her how he felt.

God how he loved her and he didn't give a damn what anyone said.

Callie slammed into her loft and paced back and forth, so freaking mad she wanted to chew nails. Jack, agitated by her mood, pranced into the kitchen, then back into the living room. "Aaaarrrggghhhh!" she shouted. "I'll show her. I'll show them all." She pulled out her cell. "Harper, I need your help."

"With what?"

"Operation Glamourpuss. Bring the big guns!"

In twenty minutes, people started to arrive at her door, some with dresses, a hairdresser, makeup artists, shoe people, nail people and finally Harper herself.

"Let's go," she said.

Callie scrubbed herself so hard in the shower, she was glowing when she came out. Celeste wanted war, she was going to get it. She was going to show that bitch, the *Scoop*, and all of New York City that this tomboy knew how to not only be a woman, but act, dress, and outdo anyone who said differently.

She surrendered herself to Harper's control. The woman smiling like a fiend. "No one messes with our girl."

Her hair was dried, makeup applied, nails and toes buffed and polished. When Harper brought out the dresses, Callie shook her head. "Nope. I already know which one I'm going to wear."

Twenty minutes later, she got out of Harper's limo, blew her a kiss and started toward the front door. Cameras went off and Callie grinned. Kiss my gorgeous ass, she thought. Celeste came out, a box in her hands, her eyes stricken. She stared at Callie for a moment, then scowled. Without a word, she bumped past her and out into the street.

Looked like Owen fired her. Served her right for not understanding that he was hers and she was his. She pulled open the door and strode inside.

She searched the club and finally saw Owen standing near the stage looking like he'd lost his best friend. But he hadn't lost her. He would never lose her.

He saw her coming toward him, and he broke away from the conversation, fighting through the crowd. "Callie!" he said. He stared at her for an instant, then he closed his eyes and hauled her into his arms, his unchecked strength nearly crushing her. He didn't say anything for the longest time, he just held on to her as if he couldn't let her go, and Callie closed her eyes and clung to him, so full of what they had together.

Finally, he let the air out of his lungs, and with unsteady fingers, he toyed with her curls. "I thought you were done with this...with me."

"No. I just had to prove a point," she said, never so sure of anything in her life. If this was what Owen needed, then she would be there one hundred percent. She'd freaking shoehorn her way in because she was fitting in no matter what. "I can do this. I can do this every day if you want me to. What's getting dolled up in pretty dresses and kickin' shoes compare to losing you? There is no comparison," she whispered, a smile filling her face. "I love you, Owen. I love you so much."

He inhaled roughly and slid his fingers around the back of her head. "I love you, too. So much, babe." He took another breath, then continued, his voice so strained, so thick with emotion that she could barely hear him. "I think we're in total agreement about that."

A thousand feelings washed through her, and she pressed her face into the hollow of his throat. Owen stroked her back, molding her closer, his touch firm and reassuring. "I'm so ready for those picket fences," he whispered unevenly.

She tightened her arms around his neck and nodded, focusing on the warm scent of him, the weight of his arms around her. Those were real and solid. And secure. He held her for a long time, rubbing her back again and tipped her face up. He gazed at her, his expression taut and solemn, then bent his head and kissed her—one of those long, wet, openmouthed kisses that made her senses swim and her body go weak. And Callie sank into it so happy, so complete. She was never going to let him go.

Steve's voice boomed over the microphone. "Hey, Owen. Let go of your beautiful girlfriend, my friend. We have an announcement to deliver!"

Dragging his mouth away, Owen pressed his face against her neck and hugged her. "I've got to go for a bit. Be prepared to head to Australia when this is done."

She nodded and kissed him. "Go," she murmured.

He backed up then, said, "Callie, you look awesome."

She laughed, hugging herself, her throat so tight she couldn't respond.

Owen walked up on the stage, his eyes scanning the crowd. He brought the microphone to his lips. "Ladies and gentlemen. Thank you so much for coming out today and sharing this moment with us." His eyes found hers, warm lights and a secretive message just for her. "I have just woken up from this self-imposed dream. I've grown and changed in the last months. It was my intention to announce today that I would be opening up two new clubs. One in LA and the other in Miami. But that's not the case now."

There was a rumbling murmur from the crowd, his three backers frowning, glances exchanged between them.

"I was taught about humility, integrity, and doing the right thing from my great aunt Matilda. She took me in when I desperately needed that in my life. I was a kid on the street, homeless. I recently stumbled on the building where I used to live, huddled in the dark and cold. I've purchased that building and am going to convert it into a community center and a shelter for children. It's going to be named: The Matilda McKay Center after her." He dropped his head for a moment and Callie's heart squeezed. She knew he was thinking about her right now. "The only club I'm opening is the one in LA."

The music started up. "You'll find the plans for it upstairs in the VIP area. Don't worry. You'll all get a chance to see it. Now, have fun!"

He walked off the stage, and Callie moved toward him as his three backers converged on him. "What is this about, Owen?" Steve growled.

"It was just one club too many and I'm going to be backing it myself. Thank you for everything, but I'm not going to need any capital." He left them and wrapped his arm around her. "Come on, babe. Let's dance."

Hours later, she let herself back into her loft. They had talked about Australia all the way back home. Callie was adamant they shouldn't leave until Jill gave birth. Owen agreed. She was going to change, wash her face, and talk to him about their upcoming trip. She had just set down her keys when she heard a terrible pounding at her door.

When she opened it, it was Owen. His eyes were frantic. He grabbed her upper arms. "Jill is having her puppies."

"What? No! It's too early."

"Only by a week. Please help her. She looks like she's having a hard time."

Without hesitation, she headed towards Owen's. door Jack whimpered when she closed him into her loft. "Sorry, buddy, but you'll just get in the way."

Callie rushed after Owen and burst inside. Hurrying up to Jill's whelping box, where the poor thing was panting and whimpering, she knelt down inside. "How's my pretty girl?" she asked softly.

The dog looked up at her with pain-filled eyes and whimpered again. Callie gently put her hand on Jill's stomach. Owen hovered over her.

"Owen, go boil water."

"Water," he said dumbfounded, not taking his eyes off Jill.

"Yes, water. Now! We need hot water and some rags. Give me your cell."

After handing her the phone, he disappeared into the kitchen. Callie dialed Poe's number. Her sleepy voice answered.

"I need your help. Jill is whelping, and she's in distress."

"I'm on my way."

Owen came back into the room and paced. Callie let him. She tried to put her feelings aside for the sake of the dog. But she couldn't help caring about Owen.

"Please help her. I can't lose her. I love that dog."

Callie's heart twisted in her chest and she rose and put her arms around him. "I'll do everything I can. Poe is on her way. Everything will be fine. First time births can be difficult."

He pulled her tight against him and said, "Callie—"

The knock at the door cut him off. "That's Poe." Callie raced to the door and pulled it open. Poe, still in her pajamas burst in. "Did you start water?"

"Done." Just then the kettle started to whistle. Owen left the room.

"Keep the water coming," Callie called after him.

Poe pushed up her sleeves and quickly and quietly examined the dog. Her face was concerned, but not overly so. Callie was already relieved, because she knew Poe was too expressive to hide it if she was really worried.

"You look amazing. I'd say the *Scoop* can go screw themselves," Poe whispered.

"Yes. I was caught off guard, but everything is going great. I'm in love with Owen."

"Well, duh—" Poe stopped talking then said, "She's having contractions, and I think she might need a little bit of help. Could you talk to her and hold her head?"

Callie got into position as Owen brought in a big bowl of water and some old towels. He set it down within Poe's reach and stepped back, watching them.

Poe dislodged the first puppy and as soon as she did, it began to yip. Poe smiled and said, "A feisty little guy. Owen, clean him off with the water and set him near Jill. She'll be worried if he's out of her sight, so stay close."

He took the wriggling little dark wet bundle of fur and ears and did as he was instructed. Callie met his eyes and the wonder in them was touching. He smiled and held the puppy close to Jill. "Look, Jill, you're a mom."

Poe was pulling out another puppy; this one was black and white—a mantle like Jill with a tiny black nose and paw pads. "It's another male." Owen set down the first male and took the latest puppy from Poe. Callie stroked Jill's head and murmured to her. "Good job. Two so far."

Over the next fifteen minutes, Poe delivered a merle black and white patterned male, two more black and white puppies, one a male and one a female, and a merle female. Poe felt her stomach and frowned. "I think there's one more."

When Callie saw the tiny Harlequin emerge, she smiled, but it soon faded as Poe looked down at it.

"Callie..." she trailed off.

"No," Callie said softly, reaching out. She took the still puppy into her hands and gently massaged. "Come on. You can do it." Her voice was clogged with tears.

The puppy gave a jerk and then started yipping. Relief swept through her. "Oh, thank God."

Poe sat back and grinned, taking the puppy from Callie and checking its sex. "It's a female."

Owen reached out and grasped her forearm. "Thank you for coming. Thank you so much!"

Poe nodded and patted his hand absently. "Let's get them to nurse, and then everything should be fine. I want to make sure the little Harlequin is okay and is nursing well before I leave."

All the puppies latched on and began drinking. Jill recovered from her labor and started licking them. At first the little Harlequin had a tough time with it, but once Poe expelled some of the milk, she latched on and started sucking.

"She looks okay, all pink and white and black. Keep them warm and let Jill take care of them. I see that you have a very nice cozy whelping box." Poe dislodged a blanket and she peered beneath it. "Callie, isn't that your Judith Leiber clutch?"

"It is? Do you suppose that's the pillow and quilt from the two other tenants?"

"Yup, and looks like there's the dinosaur quilt you told me about, Callie. Owen, apparently, your dog was nesting," Poe said. Cute girl."

Owen shook his head. "Jill was the thief?"

Poe rose and went to clean up. When she came back, she gave Owen instructions. "Now you guys are free to talk. I do think you have more than puppies to discuss." She squeezed Callie's shoulder. "Call me if you need me."

Callie nodded. She hadn't moved from Jill's head. When the door closed behind Poe, Owen turned towards her.

"Callie," he stepped forward, "We're going to have to postpone that trip for a while."

Callie rose and walked over to him. "So we are. They are so damn cute."

"It'll give us plenty of time to plan. We're doggie parents," he said with a laugh. "I love you. Love you. Love—"

She cut him off with a hard, fast kiss. Which led to another longer, slower kiss. "The feeling is so mutual, mister. The Center, that is a beautiful tribute to your great aunt."

"I'm sure she knows and is smiling right now." He took her into his arms. "We have a dilemma, or actually two."

"Oh, and they are?"

"First, love me, love my dog. And we both know she's a wanton hussy who gets into trouble when you least expect it."

"Well, with Jack in the picture, I would say that guarantees there will be more puppies in the future."

"Promise me the births will be easier. Although the fact that you have a vet on call makes that a little easier to handle. And, as long as your parents take the litters, that will be fine with me. In fact, could your parents take this litter? I don't know what I was thinking. All these Danes in this loft would make it very crowded."

"I promise. As soon as they can be moved. And what's your second dilemma?"

"I don't want you across the hall. I want you here, with me."

"Is that so?"

He nodded and kissed her again.

She smiled then. "Well, isn't it handy then that my brother had already developed a plan for knocking through that wall over there and making this loft and my loft into one?"

"That sounds like an even better plan." He traced his fingers down along her nose, and across her lips. It made her sigh and tingle all at the same time. "We'll need the space for three Great Danes."

"Three?"

"Yes, I saw the way you looked at that little Harlequin. It was love at first sight. I bet you even have a name for her."

"I do, Mr. Smarty."

"Let's hear it."

"Golden Diamond Girl's Miracle."

"Nice. And her call name?"

"I was thinking…Tilly."

He blinked rapidly and she watched as he struggled with his emotions. Finally, he nodded. "That's freaking perfect."

She laughed as he scooped her up and carried her out of the living room, then thrilled at the rascally bad-boy grin on his face as he opened the door with his hip.

"You know we have responsibilities now," he said before tossing her lightly onto the bed and landing next to her. He swiftly divested them both of their clothes, took care of protection, and pulled her under him, as they grinned at each other like a couple of silly, out-of-control, lovesick loons or…dogs.

"Yes, but we can check on them a little later," she gasped as goose bumps rushed up her arms and pebbled her nipples. Wow. Just from feeling his weight on her.

He nipped her earlobe and looked down into her eyes, then lifted her hips as he slid deep inside. "Sounds like we have a plan."

EPILOGUE

TWO WEEKS LATER

"YOU CAN'T KIDNAP someone, Harper. I have things to do."

She gave Callie a smug grin. "Oh, I can. I already did. Besides, it's a surprise."

"I don't like surprises."

"You'll like this one." Brooke and Poe said in unison, then looked at each other and locked their pinkies. "Jinx."

Callie sat back in Harper's limo, folding her arms. There was no arguing with Manhattan's Darling or her bona fide lifelong friends. When they pulled up to a glass and concrete building, Harper got out of the limo. She marched into the lobby and into the elevator in a cloud of attitude and expensive perfume.

Callie followed, her curiosity piqued. But when they got off the elevator and she saw the business name on the glass, she put on the breaks. "Oh, no, Harper."

Harper just gave her an evil grin. "Oh, yes, Callie."

She breezed through the door and stopped at the front desk. The woman gaped at her, then at them. Then back at Harper.

"You're Callie Lassiter."

Callie covered her face and groaned.

And, Harper Sinclair."

"Well, yes, I am. Thank you for noticing. I need to speak with whomever is in charge here."

"That would be the Editor in Chief, Jeffrey Dalton."

Harper looked down the hall, then raised her brows. "Office, dear. Come on, keep up."

"Oh, down the hall, first door on the left." She looked at Callie and smiled. "I loved your sequined jersey dress," she gushed. She looked around. "And, everything else you wore. You have a great sporty chic style."

Poe and Brooke giggled.

There was no way for Callie to escape. Brooke had her right arm and Poe had her left. "Thanks," she said as they marched her along with them.

Callie closed her eyes, breathing deep. Harper didn't even break stride. She burst through the *New York Scoop's* editor's door like Teddy Roosevelt taking the hill, but in Harper's case, she didn't need to walk softly or carry a big stick. The woman was a force of nature.

"Mr. Dalton?" The bespeckled man behind the desk, looked up at her, blinking.

"Who are you people?" He squinted at them. "Wait a minute. You're Harper Sinclair and you're Callie Lassiter."

"I am and she is. You will as of right now stop following her and taking pictures of her. Am I making myself clear?"

"With all due respect, ma'am. I don't take orders from you, and we're protected by the First Amendment. Photographing both of you is a very lucrative business. So you can all take your shapely asses out of my office before I call security."

"See," Brooke said. "I was right."

"She was," Poe agreed, nodding.

"You're a short-sighted man printing a gossip paper. And, you're going to take orders from me and my shapely ass."

"Oh, why is that?" he scoffed, the phone in his hand.

"I bought this rag and am now the new owner." She raised her brows and gave him a nasty smile. "That means I'm now your boss."

The look on his face was priceless as he hung up his phone. Callie's laughter could be heard all the way down the hall.

TWO MONTHS LATER

"Are you sure she's ready for this?" Owen asked as Callie walked with him, Jack, and Jill toward the fenced in area that held all the equipment for Jill's training. They had just returned from Australia and were rested and relaxed before they had to go back to work. She'd never forget how wonder it was to scuba dive with Owen, sharing in the memories of The Great Barrier Reef. Also, the center was almost complete and Owen would be dedicating it soon. He'd purchased a building in LA and was just about to give the go ahead on the renovations. Everything was progressing smoothly, including their plans to combine their two lofts. Ian was busy working with Owen, thrilled to put his plan into action.

"Yes, Poe's given her the go ahead. The puppies are thriving here at Lassiter Run. This has been so fun to put together. She's going to be great at agility. I know it."

They reached the area and Owen set his forearms on the fence. "It all looks daunting to me."

She kissed him on his cheek. "Well, it's a good thing then that it's Jill who's going to be doing all the hard work."

He laughed and caught her around the neck and turned her into the fence, her back against the slats. "Did I tell you that I love you today?"

"Several times, but you were making love to me, so maybe it was the pleasure talking. You can tell me again if you must," she said in a bored tone.

Smiling into her eyes, he reached up and grabbed a handful of hair and drew her toward him. Trapping her against him and the fence, he said, "Don't look now but you're between me and a white fence. It's not exactly a picket one, but it's close."

She gave him a dry steady look. "It will do," she said, grinning. A symbol to our domesticated bliss?"

"Yeah, you almost blissed me to death this morning." His gaze warm and intimate, he stared at her, his eyes alive with delight. "It was a hell of a way to wake up."

"Who needs an alarm clock, and I forgot to tell you what a nice ass you have."

He caught her by the back of the head and tightened his hold, his embrace so solid and warm. "I love you like hell, babe," he said, his voice husky and uneven.

Her jaw locked against the overwhelming feelings for him, and she pressed her face into his neck, absorbing his strength and warmth.

He released a heavy sigh and smoothed his hand over her hair, then kissed her forehead.

Jack barked, then Jill joined in, nudging him as if she was eager to start working on all that equipment behind them.

"Looks like we've got us some pushy dogs."

"Hey, don't say a thing against them," she mock scolded. "If they hadn't gotten it on, we might have never realized how perfect we were for each other." They looked down at the two dogs.

"Thanks, you guys." Jack barked again and pranced around. Jill mimicking him.

"A beautiful doggie you're welcome." She kissed Owen then opened the gate. "Come on then. Let's see what you have, girl."

Once inside, she tied Jack's leash to the fence. "Take off her collar and leash." She rubbed her hands together. Before she could even give Jill a command, she was hurtling the jumps and going through the tunnel. She grinned at Owen. "Looks like she's a natural."

He laughed and ran out there, the sun shining on his hair and in the dogs' coats.

SIX MONTHS LATER

Callie was in the stands watching Owen and Jill compete in their very first agility competition. Tilly was thriving and growing into a beautiful, albeit smaller-sized Great Dane, and the construction on their loft was complete. She and her three friends, her parents, and her brother were all yelling their fool heads off.

Jill moved quickly but surely as Owen ran beside her and gave her the hand signals. The clock on the leader board ticked along. She was so close...yes! She beat the time. As Callie clapped, the leader board changed and for a moment she stared as she saw her name. *Callie, will you marry me?*

Harper squealed and hugged her. She watched in stunned amazement as Owen and Jill trotted up to her. He stopped and sent Jill the rest of the way. She had a turquoise bag in her mouth. Inside the bag, Callie found a turquoise ring box. With shaking hands, she opened it to reveal the most beautiful ring. A round cut diamond with little diamonds all around it, the setting a brushed platinum.

She looked up to find Owen standing there. The audience watched them. "You asked me to marry you at your first competition?"

"Yes. In front of all these people, your family, and friends. I want the whole world to know you're mine. I love you, Callie."

He took the ring out of the box and slipped it on her finger. "It's perfect for working with dogs," she said. "No chance of it snagging on collars."

"Exactly. A sporty ring for my girl-next-door."

Jill woofed and everyone laughed as Callie threw her arms around Owen.

She whispered in his ear, "I love you, too, and my answer is yes!"

Then she kissed him. Right in front of a whole stadium full of very interested and amused people.

Don't miss the story of Brooke Palmer's romance and the chaos of Callie's wedding plans in the next Going to the Dogs Series – Groomed.

GROOMED

Can a dog have a bad hair day?

Brooke Palmer owns Pawlish, an exclusive doggie spa and grooming business in upper Manhattan, but when a client's champion poodle gets a bad poodle cut and has to undergo therapy to recover, the client sues. The lawyer they send is drop dead gorgeous, but Brooke won't be wooed by a corporate shark in a sharp suit.

Corporate lawyer Drew Hudson has better things to do then take on this ridiculous lawsuit, but since he works for the client's husband, he has no choice. After meeting the beautiful, sweet-tempered owner, he can't keep his mind on the silly case. But when the client turns up dog gone dead, Brooke may be a conflict of interest when she's charged with the murder. All Drew wants to do is prove that this sexy entrepreneur is not dangerous, except to his heart.

Can she take a chance on him?

OTHER TITLES BY ZOE DAWSON

ROMANTIC COMEDY
Going to the Dogs series
Leashed #1, Groomed #2
Hounded #3, Collared #4
Piggy Bank Blues #5, Holding Still #6
Louder Than Words #7

Going to the Dogs Wedding Novellas
Fetched #1, Tangled #2
Handled #3, Captured #4
Novellas (the complete series)

NEW ADULT
Hope Parish Novels
A Perfect Mess #1, A Perfect Mistake #2
A Perfect Dilemma #3, Resisting Samantha #4
Handling Skylar #5, Sheltering Lawson #6

Hope Parish Novellas
Finally Again #1, Beauty Shot #2
Mark Me #3, Novellas 1-3 (the complete series)
A Perfect Wedding #4, A Perfect Holiday #5
A Perfect Question #6, Novellas 4-6 (the complete series)

Maverick Allstars series
Ramping Up #1

SMALL TOWN
Laurel Falls series
Leaving Yesterday #1

URBAN FANTASY
The Starbuck Chronicles
AfterLife #1

EROTICA
Forbidden Plays series
Playing Rough #1, Hard Pass #2, Illegal Motions #3